Million Dollar Mates

Catwalk Queen

More Million Dollar Mates books

Million Dollar Mates
Paparazzi Princess

And, coming soon . . .

Golden Girl

Other series by Cathy Hopkins

Mates, Dates
Truth, Dare, Kiss or Promise
Cinnamon Girl
Zodiac Girls

Cathy Hopkins

Million Dollar Mates

Catwalk Queen

SIMON AND SCHUSTER

First published in Great Britain in 2011
by Simon and Schuster UK Ltd.
A CBS COMPANY

Simon & Schuster UK Ltd
1st Floor
222 Gray's Inn Road
London WC1X 8HB

This book is a work of fiction. Names, characters, places and
incidents are either the product of the author's imagination
or are used fictitiously. Any resemblance to actual people
living or dead, events or locales is entirely coincidental.

A CIP catalogue record for this book is
available from the British Library.

978-1-84738-759-2

1 3 5 7 9 10 8 6 4 2

Printed and bound in Great Britain by
CPI Cox & Wyman, Reading RG1 8EG

www.simonandschuster.co.uk
www.cathyhopkins.com

1

New Arrival

'I wonder who it is,' I said to Pia, as we stood huddled in our coats and scarves round the back of Number 1, Porchester Park and watched a ton of gilt furniture being carried to the lift inside. We'd just returned from school and when we saw the trucks, we thought we'd go round and have a nose about instead of heading straight home. It was a cold February afternoon and a new resident was moving in. All very hush hush. I'd tried to get it out of Dad. He'd know exactly who it was, seeing as he was general manager of the place, but, as usual, when it came to the residents, he was giving nothing away.

'They've got exotic taste, that's for sure,' said Pia, as the removal men carried a velvet leopard print chaise longue past while other men struggled by with a giant marble pillar. '*Footballers' Wives* meets Hollywood. Very *Hello* magazine. You must have *some* idea, Jess.'

I shook my head. 'Nada. Honest. I'm not sure that Dad trusts me not to blab to someone I shouldn't.'

'Text Alisha. She might know.'

'Good idea,' I said. I got out my phone and sent a message. Alisha is the daughter of Afro-American actor, Jefferson Lewis. She lives in one of the penthouse suites at the top of Porchester Park and is our mate.

She replied instantly: **Come up.**

She's home-schooled so is often longing for a bit of company around this time of day.

'Did your dad tell you anything?' asked Pia as we made our way back to the staff area then headed into the residents' part, where we stood for a moment to let the security camera scan our irises before the door opened to let us through. The type of people who live here are hot on security, so the whole system was designed by the SAS – bulletproof windows and all.

'You know what Dad's like. I just overheard the end

of a conversation and he was saying we could expect the paparazzi to be camped outside for a while when she arrives.'

'Ah. So we know the new resident is a she!' said Pia.

'That's true. No doubt we'll find out who soon enough.'

We crossed the marble-floored reception and gave Grace at the desk a wave. She nodded back. She never questioned where we were going any more. Everyone who worked at Number 1 knew that Pia and I were friends with Alisha. As Pia pressed the lift button, I had a look at the flower display on the centre table today. Tall white orchids. Very elegant and, as always, the air smelt perfumed from the Jo Malone wild fig and cassis candles that were constantly burning there.

The lift doors swished open to let us into the mirrored interior. Pia grimaced at her reflection as we stepped inside and pressed the button for the penthouse suite.

'I look so pale,' she said. 'I think I'll get a spray tan.'

'Me too. Whiter than white,' I said. It wasn't surprising. The temperature outside was below zero and had been for some days. It had even snowed yesterday.

3

I pulled out my plait so my hair was loose and Pia applied some berry lipgloss. We always feel we need to make an effort when we go up to the Lewises'. It's so glamorous up there: the family, the apartment, the air. I'm not kidding, even the air smells expensive. I find it hard sometimes, the 'us and them' situation, upstairs-downstairs. The type of people who live in the apartments are seriously rich. They have to be as the apartments start at nineteen million pounds and go up to a hundred and fifty. I live with my dad, my brother Charlie and my cat Dave in one of the five mews houses for staff, which are sited round the back. They're nothing special. Modern houses, clean and light with Ikea furniture. Pia lives in one of them too – her mum runs the spa at Porchester Park. We've made the most of our rooms; mine's turquoise and deep lavender and Pia's is done in Indian colours – bright pink, orange and red – but they're nothing compared to the apartments upstairs, where they don't have art prints framed on the wall, they have original paintings by grand masters and the decorators' bills alone could buy our mews house about ten times over. Our lifestyles are so different. Like Pia and I get fifteen quid pocket money a week, while Alisha has three credit cards and permission to spend. She dresses in Tommy Hilfiger and Prada, while Pia and I can barely afford Topshop. Alisha has her curly shoulder-length hair blow-dried to a shiny gloss every day. Pia and I sometimes have to cut each other's hair because we're so broke. We travel on the bus, Alisha goes by limo. We get on, though. We do. Even though she's from a rich family, mates are very important to her. Just some days it gets to me – the A-lister lifestyle and all that goes with it seems way out of my league and my life so ordinary in comparison.

'What's up?' asked Pia.

'Nothing. Why?'

'You've got that look on your face, like you're worried about something.'

'No. OK, yes. OK, I don't know.'

Pia laughed. 'So that's clear, then.'

I could never keep anything hidden from Pia, partly because I'm one of those unlucky people who doesn't seem able to disguise what I'm feeling – everything shows on my face – but Pia can also read me. We've been friends so long we can finish each other's sentences and often know what the other is thinking.

'Is it JJ?' Pia asked. 'Or Alexei, or Tom?'

The boys in my life.

JJ is Alisha's older, well fit, handsome, lovely brother. A Hunky McDunky. I used to think I was in with a chance with him but lately I'm not sure. As I've got to know him and the whole Lewis family better, I've had more chances to observe him and I can see that he's charming to everyone. We swim together two nights a week in the spa and I'd been hoping that something might happen, but when we've done our lengths, he leaves me to go and shower upstairs. Probably a good thing because wet hair dripping down my back is *not* my best look.

Alexei is new to Porchester Park. His family moved in a few weeks ago. He's heart-stoppingly beautiful, blond and perfect. He's cool, too. He wants to meet people his own age so asked me if I could introduce him to my friends. I'm not sure how I feel about him yet. Star-struck, mainly, as he really is gorgeous and although he's not a star, he has the charisma of one. I've spoken to him a few times and, like JJ, he's very charming and polite. I'm not sure he's the One for me, though, as I don't get the same rush when he looks into my eyes as I do when JJ does, but I've not ruled him out because sometimes love grows.

And, lastly, Tom. He's in the Sixth Form and is the school babe magnet. He's about as opposite as you could get in looks to JJ, who always looks neat, like he's just stepped out of a shower, his hair short, his dress style casual but preppy smart. Tom's look is dishevelled with unkempt longish hair like he's just rolled out of bed – and he dresses like he's picked his clothes up off the floor – but he's sexy as hell. He could have anyone he wanted and he knows it – he loves to flirt and doesn't do commitment. After a few close encounters of the snogging kind, he's doing my head in. Lately, due to my confidence collapse (only a quarter of which I'd confessed to Pia, in case I got a lecture), I felt it was never going to happen with him. It seems to be going that way with everyone I like. I'm sure it's because I'm ordinary, ordinary, ordinary, bland, bland, bland, boring, boring. I even bore *myself* some days.

'I guess,' I replied. 'I mean, look at me, Pia. Why would boys like JJ or Alexei even give me a second chance?'

'Because you're fun to hang out with and you're stunning.'

I glanced at my reflection as the lift reached the Lewises' floor. I saw a tall girl with chestnut-brown hair and blue eyes. Average build, average looks. Ordinary. *Not* stunning.

'No, I'm not. You're the pretty one.'

Pia slapped me lightly on the arm. 'You're so down on yourself. Stop it!'

'Bleurgh,' I groaned and pulled my tongue out at myself as we stepped out of the lift.

Pia missed the self-doubt gene when they were handing out personalities, whereas I got a double helping. She always gives me a telling-off if I'm negative about myself but I'm right about one thing, she *is* the pretty one – small, curvy, with dark hair and a face that's full of life and mischief. She has a great sense of style too – a bit vintage, with strong colours and big accessories that I'd never wear – like the huge amber fly ring she's wearing today. All my friends have their own style: Flo is willowy and tall, a romantic dreamer who dresses in soft pastels and floaty clothes, like a Pre-Raphaelite princess, and Meg always wears great tailored clothes with a military slant. I'm the ordinary one. I dress in jeans and T-shirts – all perfectly acceptable but I don't have my own look that stands out from the crowd like they all do.

Alisha was waiting for us when we got up to the penthouse. She looked fabulous in perfect-fitting jeans, a red top and red Converse. Even she had her own look, although her clothes weren't that different from mine, they just fitted better and were in the best fabrics – cashmere or silk – so looked expensive.

'Hey, peeps,' she said, as she closed the door behind us.

'Hey, peeps,' we replied in fake American accents. She laughed and led us towards the kitchen where their housekeeper, Marguerite, was preparing mango smoothies. She knew they were our favourite. I settled myself on a stool at the black granite breakfast bar. The Lewises' kitchen is as big as the ground floor of our house with an amazing view of Hyde Park through floor-to-ceiling windows. Everything in there is scaled up: a huge American fridge with a range of fresh juices from cranberry to elderflower, a cooker big enough to cook for an army on, a long glass dining table that could seat twelve and sofas round a coffee table with an enormous TV screen in the wall at the far end. The first time I saw it, I was awestruck, but now I feel quite at home. I like the whole apartment. No doubt the décor is all mega expensive but it's homely too and there's always something yummy-smelling baking. I've seen a few of the other apartments at Porchester Park and some of them have an unlived-in feel, all cold marble and empty gleaming surfaces, but the Lewis style is chic and comfy, with cushions, books, artefacts, big abstract paintings and rugs everywhere.

Once the drinks were in front of us, the housekeeper made herself scarce and we could talk.

'So, what's new, guys?' Alisha asked. 'What's the goss from school?'

Pia shrugged. 'Same ole from the teachers: boring. Boring. Important year. Exams. Work harder. Tons of homework. Yada yada yada.'

'Any sign of Tom?' asked Alisha.

I shook my head. 'I see him around but he's keeping himself distant.'

'Ah, the dance,' said Alisha.

'What dance?'

'You show you're interested in a boy, he steps back. You cool off like you don't care, he steps forward.'

'Sounds about right. Time to dance backwards.' I got off the stool and did a backwards moonwalk and almost fell over the coffee table. Alisha and Pia laughed. 'Seriously, though, I think that if I'm to be in with a chance with any boy I like then I need to do something to stand out from the crowd.'

Pia drained her drink. 'You do stand out,' she said. Ever my champion. 'Doesn't she, Alisha?'

Alisha looked doubtful.

'See, even Alisha agrees with me,' I said.

'No, I don't,' said Alisha, 'but I see where you're coming from. You're good-looking, yeah, but sometimes that's not enough for a boy.'

'Make 'em laugh, that's what I say,' said Pia.

'Yeah but *with* you, not at you,' I said.

'Basically it's chemistry, I reckon,' said Alisha. 'The spark's either there or not.'

I'm not so sure. There's a spark there with Tom. Definitely. I know he's felt it too. He just doesn't want a relationship. I've felt a spark with JJ too but, so far, he's made no move to take it further. And Alexei's hard to read. There's not exactly a spark with him but he's the one who seems the most interested and acts like he wants to see more of me. Thing is, he always asks about my friends and says how he'd like to meet them. I'm not sure if I'm just a ticket to meet other girls and that's why he's being nice. I know from Alisha that it can be hard for the teen residents at Porchester Park to meet people. Like her and JJ, many of them are home-schooled, and don't get the interaction that Pia and I do. So, there they are. JJ. Tom. Alexei. Three high-flyers in their own ways. And then there's me. Jess Hall. An ordinary teen. A schoolgirl and swimming champion, but that doesn't

11

exactly make me hot. I often ask myself why I can't fall for one of the ordinary boys at school, maybe one of my classmates or a boy in the next year up. They're not out of my league. I've seen a few of them checking me out, like Adrian Neilson in Year Eleven. Why can't I fall for him? Because he smells of stale socks and old cheese, that's why. No. My love arrow seems to be aiming high and I need to do something to raise myself out of the realms of the average.

'And, anyway, I thought you liked my brother,' said Alisha.

'I do but—'

'Hey, Alisha, do you know who's moving in yet?' asked Pia, as she finished her drink. I think she sensed we were getting into a sensitive area, because with JJ being so close to Alisha, I hadn't told her the full story about how I really felt – not that I was totally clear about it myself!

'I do,' Alisha replied.

'And?'

Alisha grinned. 'Guess.'

Pia sighed impatiently. 'I don't know. The Queen. Madonna. Posh Spice. It's Posh, isn't it?'

Alisha looked at me. 'You want to guess?'

'Er . . . a woman?'

Alisha nodded.

'An actress?'

'Maybe. I think she's done a bit of acting as well as other things.'

'Oh just *tell* us, Alisha,' said Pia. 'Stop doing the *X Factor* judge act on us.'

'OK. She arrives this evening. And it's . . . Tanisha.'

'No way! Tanisha! Tanisha as in *the* Tanisha?' I gasped.

Alisha nodded. 'Tanisha.'

Ohmigod! Only the biggest best most famous awesome stunning pop diva in the entire world. I loved her. I loved her music. I'd had posters of her on my wall when I lived at Gran's. And she was coming to live at Porchester Park! I might get to see her going in and out. I might even get to meet her. Suddenly it didn't matter about JJ or Tom or Alexei. I was going to be living in close proximity to one of my all-time idols.

2
Blast from the Past

'Two messages,' I said as I glanced at my Facebook page.

After Alisha's, Pia and I had gone back to my house and up to my room to Google Tanisha on my computer. There were millions of pages about her! On-stage, in magazines, at award ceremonies. When we'd finished looking, I'd gone onto Facebook to see if I had any messages. There were two and one friend request. I clicked on the first message.

Hi Jess. I'm back from Australia. Let's meet.
All feels new here, even though I've only been

gone four years. Seems a lot has changed plus
new school for me. Be good to catch up with
someone I used to know. KO X

K.O. Keira Oakley. I felt cold just seeing her name.

I quickly clicked on the second message. It was
from Alexei. We'd added each other as friends the
day after we met.

Hope to see you soon Jess, and meet your
friends, Alexei.

'Ve love your Russian vays and vant to be your friend,'
said Pia in a terrible Russian accent.

'I do,' I said with a sigh, 'but it's as clear as day right
there in his message, he doesn't want to just see me,
he vants to meet my friends. Do you fancy him?'

Pia shook her head. 'I don't know. I haven't met
him yet but I have seen him and he's not my type. I
mean, he's beautiful, yes. Graceful even, like a ballet
dancer, but I'm not that mad on blond boys. No, I like
my rough, tough, old bruiser boy.' She meant Henry
who, with his dark stocky looks, is more rugby player
than ballet dancer. He also lives in the staff area at
Porchester Park. His dad looks after the fleet of cars

15

in the basement car park. Pia's been dating him since she moved in and they're like an old married couple with their regular dates; hanging out at each other's houses; daily, sometimes hourly, texts. Pia's love life has always been uncomplicated. Since she was twelve, she's had three relationships with three great boys: Jake, Dave and Henry (who she's with now) who didn't play games or have issues about commitment. She only broke up with the first two because Jake's family moved to Canada and she and Dave decided that although they loved each other, they weren't *in* love. They've stayed good mates, all the same. I haven't even had one proper boyfriend because I always pick boys who don't know what they want or don't want a relationship.

I messaged back that Alexei should come on Thursday evening as Meg and Flo would be over. I couldn't refuse to introduce him to them, it would be mean, but I didn't feel happy about it. When I first saw Alexei, I thought it was love at first sight but really it was awe at first sight. I hadn't spent long enough with him to know if we would really get on or even if he was fun to be with. It's too soon to ask the others to steer clear and say he's MINE, all MINE, but what if one of them falls for him? Or what if we really hit it off and then Tom or JJ suddenly want to be with me? It's so difficult. *Why can't I be like Pia and have three boyfriends that come along one after the other*, I thought, *Not three boys who come along all at the same time and leave me not knowing what's going on with any of them!* Whatever the outcome, I've decided that I have to be cool with all of them and not let on that I'm interested because boys, especially ones like Tom, like a challenge.

I went to Keira's profile but couldn't see much because I hadn't added her as a friend yet. Her profile picture was a cartoon fox wearing a tiara so I couldn't even see what she looked like now.

Pia squeezed next to me on the chair at my desk. 'You don't have to add her as a friend, you know,' she said, as she glanced at the screen.

'Yes, but she'll know if I don't and why shouldn't I? I mean, I have hundreds of friends on Facebook. Another can't hurt.'

'Another like Kiera Oakley could,' said Pia. 'Don't you remember what we used to say? KO, the opposite of OK. Anyway, the number of friends you have isn't a competition.'

'I know.' I kept meaning to go through my friends on Facebook and take off the people I hardly knew. When

I first joined, like everyone else, it was a frenzy to see how many friends I could get up to. Now, a year on, I'm not so sure I want everyone seeing my private photos and status updates. Pia's been through and thinned hers down to her real friends. As usual, I'm worried about hurting people's feelings so still have hundreds of friends I hardly know – plus it's a buzz seeing my list grow. It makes me feel popular. But Keira? I'd always felt uncomfortable around her. We used to hang out because she lived three doors down from where I used to live when Mum was alive and was often round at our house or at my gran's when I was over there. *She might have changed,* I told myself. *Four years is a long time.*

'I remember how I felt when I first came to Porchester Park, Pia. I remember being the outsider. Keira might need friends.'

Pia pulled a face. 'Pff,' she said as I pressed to confirm Keira as a friend and messaged her back.

Sure we can meet up. Let me know when or where and welcome back to not so sunny England. Jess X

Pia looked at the screen over my shoulder and grimaced again. 'I bet she hasn't asked me to be her friend.

She always knew I'd got her measure. You're too soft-hearted, Jess.'

'It was years ago. She might have changed,' I said. Actually, part of me was intrigued by Keira. She had an edge, even felt a bit dangerous. She always used to dare me to do mad things, like one time at a sleep-over when we were about nine, she'd encouraged me to creep downstairs with her after her mum and dad had gone to bed and go and do the Highland fling on the pavement outside. Pia stayed inside but I went. I remember cars going past and drivers looking out at us as if we were bonkers. A neighbour reported us to the police, who turned up and gave us a telling-off, and Mum was well mad, saying anybody could have stopped and picked us up. Keira thought it was hysterical.

'And remember Michael,' Pia continued.

I shrugged, but I hadn't forgotten about Michael. He was my first love and she'd stolen him from me. We were only eleven but even then I knew the rules – that friends came first and that if a friend liked a boy and publicly declared it then it was hands off. Everyone knew I liked Michael Jones. I'd had a crush on him for ages but then one night, I was walking home with Pia from school and there he was, with

Keira outside her gate, and she had her arms around his neck. I watched as she kissed him, then glanced over his shoulder at me with a challenging look, like, are you going to make something of it? I felt like someone had slapped me. I didn't let on, though. Instead I stuffed my rucksack up my dress, staggered over to them and groaned, 'Michael, how could you do this to me when I'm having your baby?' They both cracked up. That was me, Jess, the good sport, what a good joke, a laugh. No-one but Pia knew I was gutted and cried for weeks after.

'That was years ago, P,' I said. 'We were kids and I wouldn't go near Michael now if you paid me. He's so full of himself and not the least bit fanciable any more so really she did me a favour and saved me from a disaster. It can't do any harm to meet up. Everyone deserves a second chance.'

'Just don't let her near the big three.'

'The big three?'

'JJ, Alexei or Tom. She'll try and get off with them just to prove that she can.'

'No reason why she'd meet them. I can go and meet her somewhere like the mall, far away from here. She's not likely to go to our school and she's not exactly likely to meet the Porchester Park residents unless I bring her back and that's not going to happen.'

Pia raised an eyebrow and gave me a knowing look. 'Your choice, but I think that girl is, and always was, bad news.'

A nagging feeling told me that Pia was right. Maybe I should have thought twice about agreeing to meet Keira but, too late, the message had already gone. *It'll be fine*, I told myself. *We'll meet, have a catch up, job done.*

The encounter came sooner than I'd reckoned. I was coming out of school the next day and there was Keira standing outside the gate. She looked amazing. She'd grown as tall as me and had great legs shown off by thick tights worn under denim shorts and paired with grey suede Ugg boots. Her dark red hair was cut into glossy layers which fell to her shoulders and showed off her heart-shaped face, great cheekbones and wide mouth that she'd painted a pillar box red. I saw a few guys from the Sixth Form check her out as they came out and I prayed that Tom wouldn't be one of them. He'd be well interested in her if he saw her. She looked one hundred per cent bad girl – just the sort of challenge he'd love.

'Hey, you,' she said, as she spotted Pia and me. She flashed a big smile at me and blanked Pia. 'I remembered where your gran lived, so I called in and she told me which school you went to now.'

'Er, yeah. Hey, Keira,' I said. 'Um. How was Australia?'

She shrugged a shoulder. 'Hot. Wild.'

Pia pushed her way forward. 'Yeah, hi, Keira. Remember me? I remember you.' She said the last part like a warning.

Keira laughed. 'So you two still hang out?'

'Best friends forever,' said Pia.

Keira gave her a fake smile. 'Aw, sweet.'

'Are you back for good?' asked Pia.

Keira shrugged again. 'For a couple of months. Mum was desperate to see her family. It's so not fair that I had to be dragged along as well just to see a load of stuffy old aunts. But at least we're back at the old house. It was only rented while we were away.'

'So you've seen some of the neighbours?' I asked.

'Some. Seems a lot's changed.'

She must have heard that my mum died just over a year ago but she didn't say anything, even though she'd known her. It didn't surprise me. I was getting used to people's different reactions. A lot of people

22

just didn't know what to say. One neighbour even crossed the street when she saw Charlie and me, rather than mention it.

'Want to grab a coffee, catch up?' she asked.

I looked at Pia. 'Can't,' she said. 'Got drama.'

'What about you, Jess?'

I'd arranged to see JJ in the spa for swimming practice but I felt myself hesitate. I didn't want to tell Keira in case she decided to tag along.

'Jess has got swimming practice at the local baths,' Pia lied for me. 'Go on, Jess, you'd better hurry. You know what Mr Bennie's like if you're late.'

'So you're still swimming?' asked Keira in a way that said, how totally uncool.

'She's the school champion,' said Pia.

'Really?' said Keira with a half-laugh. 'School champion. Well done you.'

That mocking laugh and tone of voice. It all came flooding back. Maybe she hadn't changed after all. Keira had always been able to reduce whatever I did to nothing, with just a look or a comment. If I was reading something, she'd pick up the book then give me a look as if to say, you're reading *this*? Sometimes she'd look at what I was wearing and, just with a glance, make me feel like I'd picked the wrong outfit or colours. Now I remembered, I hadn't just felt uncomfortable around her, I'd felt insignificant.

'Actually, she's brilliant,' said Pia. 'A total star.'

But Keira appeared not to be listening and was watching people pour out of school. *Please don't let Tom come out*, I prayed. *Please don't let Tom come out.* Too late, I could see his tousled head in the distance.

Pia saw him too and went into action. 'Right, got to go. You too, Jess. Bye, Kiera, nice seeing you. Why not walk to the bus stop with Jess? Yeah. Ah, there it is, your bus, Jess, better run.'

I looked behind her to see my bus approaching. I glanced over at Keira. 'I really do have to go. I'll catch you later, on Facebook, yeah?'

Behind her, I saw Pia roll her eyes and mime, '*Noooooooo.*'

Keira shrugged. 'Sure, go if you have to.' She did her half-laugh again. 'After four years, you've got to go to swim practice. Fine, you go. Whatever. See ya, Jess.'

She began to walk away in the same direction that Tom had gone. *Please, please, don't let them meet*, I thought as I ran for the bus. As I got on and took a seat, I felt bad. *Now not only do I feel uncomfortable and insignificant*, I thought, *I also feel guilty and mean and selfish.* She'd come all the way to see me. She'd made an effort. She was right. We hadn't seen each other for four years. I could have texted JJ to rearrange.

As the bus took off again, Tom spotted me looking out of the window. He blew me a kiss. *If only you meant it*, I thought. A short distance away, I saw Keira watching. She turned to see who I was looking at, just at the moment that Tom clocked her. A slow smile appeared on his face. New blood, I knew that's what he'd be thinking, but Keira turned and began to walk in the opposite direction. *Arghhh*, I thought as my bus turned the corner, *Arghh, arghh, arghh.*

3

JJ

After my swim with JJ, I got the OK to use the changing rooms from Pia's mum then quickly headed over there. They had Jo Malone products, huge white fluffy towels and walk-in state-of-the-art showers. I'd be mad not to take the opportunity to relish the luxury. The pool is for residents only. I'm the only staff relative who's officially allowed to use it and Pia and I use the changing room facilities unofficially because her mum lets us sneak in occasionally when no-one's around. Today, after my encounter with Keira, I really felt the need for some by-myself chill time to chew it all over. The fact that I'm allowed in the pool is down to JJ.

What a resident wants, a resident gets at Porchester Park and he'd wanted a swimming partner to pace him. When I was asked if I'd mind, I'd laughed – like, *mind?* No way. I felt like I'd won a prize. JJ always goes back up to his family's apartment to shower afterwards, so as soon as the place was empty, my plan was to have a beauty sesh and relax. I'd planned a long aromatic shower and hair wash then a pore cleanse in the sauna. My skin and hair really needed it. My period was due and I was feeling like Queen Blob, plus my skin was all pasty with a threatening chin spot. Not my best look for spending time with anyone, never mind a boy I fancied, so I'm glad that JJ wasn't going to be hanging about. It's OK when we're in the water because it's head down and only come up for air, and he'd be long gone by the time I emerged.

'Hey, Jess, fancy a drink?' JJ called through the changing room door.

'Wha . . .' *Oh no,* I thought as I took in my reflection in the mirrored walls. I looked like Shrek. *Nooooo.* 'Drink? You mean later? Where?'

I peeked out and JJ indicated the empty swimming area around which were a number of wooden loungers with cushions. 'Here. Now. What do you fancy and I'll put an order in.'

'I . . . Oh.' I couldn't think up an excuse fast enough. 'Um. OK. Hot chocolate, please. That would be fab.'

'OK, get a robe and see you out here in five.'

I cursed that I hadn't brought my lipgloss or any make-up and wondered whether to dash upstairs and get some. I decided not to – he'd see I'd put make-up on and it might look like I was trying too hard. I quickly dried off my hair a little, pulled it up into a ponytail, donned one of the white robes from the changing room and went back out. A drink. That was close to a date and I couldn't help but feel a rush of anticipation when I saw JJ was stretched out on one of the loungers wearing a similar robe to my own. Unlike me, he looked in great condition, like he'd just stepped out of a page of *Vogue for Men*. He patted the lounger next to him.

'What's the occasion?' I asked as I sat next to him and turned away slightly so he couldn't see just how shiny-faced I was.

'No occasion. I just wanted to hang out. We never talk much when we swim.'

'No,' I said. *Say something else, something interesting*, I told myself as I looked at his handsome face. He had lovely deep brown eyes and great cheekbones. I cursed that my brain had gone blank. I'd fantasised about this moment for so long – alone with JJ, chatting away, bowling him over with my wit – but now I couldn't think of anything to say. 'So . . . Yes. No. I guess we don't talk much. No matter. Conversation is overrated.'

JJ laughed. 'That's a line from a movie, isn't it? The hero says that then leans over and kisses the heroine.'

I felt myself redden. In fact, I could probably have heated the whole of the spa with my blush. Was he going to lean over and kiss me? No. He hadn't moved in my direction and no way did I look like the heroine from any movie except a horror film. 'A line? Is it? Not a movie I've seen, I don't think. Er . . . Cold out, isn't it?' *Argh. Shut up Jess*, I thought. *The weather. How could I talk about that? How boring. He'll think I'm so dull.*

'Yeah. Quite a change from California but it's nice to have the seasons like you do over here.' He was so polite, as always.

We sat in silence for a few minutes. My brain was doing a scan of topics to talk about. Something to make me sound sophisticated, fascinating. 'So, JJ. Do you like curry?' I blurted. *Curry! For God's sake, Jess. Nooooooo, shut up, shut up*, my mind screamed at me.

JJ burst out laughing, then gave me a quizzical look. 'Yeah, I like curry. You?'

I shook my head. 'Not really. Um. Ever been to India?'

'Actually, yes, I have. A couple of times. It's amazing. Full of colour. Everywhere you look there's a photo just waiting to be taken. You been?'

'No. I saw a programme about it once, though.' Hell. This wasn't going well. With every sentence, I was proving myself to be a loser, confirming that I was not in his world, worse than that, I was deadly boring, a person who lived through the telly instead of getting out there and experiencing life first-hand. And a person who doesn't like curry.

'How's school life?' asked JJ.

'Same ole. Lots of extra homework at the moment.'

JJ shifted on his lounger. 'Er . . . That boy Tom goes to your school, doesn't he?'

I nodded. 'Tom Robertson. Yeah. In the Sixth Form.'

'Alisha told me you liked him.'

Remind me to kill her, I thought. 'Everyone likes Tom,' I said. 'He's very popular.'

'Yeah. I met him, remember? At the swimming championship.'

'Oh yes.'

'He's very handsome.'

'Uh.'

'And he seems fun.'

'Yes.'

'And very confident. Is he with anyone at the moment?'

I wondered why he was asking about Tom and then it hit me.

Ohmigod. Of course. JJ's gay, I thought. Of course he is. He's too good to be true. Smells gorgeous. Immaculate dress sense. Charming. Sensitive . . .

But he had a girl with him on his Christmas holiday, my inner voice reminded me.

Yes but, it didn't work out. He might have just realised he's gay and it was Tom that did it. Not surprising. Oh bummer. Another good man bites the dust. Why oh why are all the good ones gay? But at least that narrows my list down to Tom or Alexei – although Tom's not really an option so Alexei it is, that is if we get on. Blimey, my mind is racing . . .

'Jess?'

'Yes?'

'Did you hear what I said?'

'Yes. No. Sorry. What did you say?'

'Is Tom your boyfriend?'

'Hell no. Tom doesn't do relationships. He has half the school after him.'

'You included?'

'Nah,' I said. 'I don't do groupie. He has enough admirers without adding me to the long list or you. Sorry to be so blunt but I'd hate to see you get hurt—'

'Me? Why me get hurt?'

I felt myself blush again. 'Oh nothing. Sorry.' I shook my head. 'Water on the brain.' Maybe JJ didn't want to admit that he was gay. Some boys didn't.

'Yeah. I've met guys like Tom. It's all about the challenge.'

'Yep,' I agreed.

'So . . . if he's not your boyfriend, what's your position?'

'Free as a bird. No-one asking me out.' Maybe I could have a good old chinwag with JJ about my sad love life and see if he had any advice to offer.

'I am.'

'You?'

'Yes.'

'But you're gay.'

JJ's mouth fell open. 'What?' he spluttered.

'It's OK. I mean, I won't tell anyone else if you're not ready to come out yet.' JJ's face looked more and more shocked. I realised I had to backtrack fast. 'We don't have to talk about it at all but I felt it only fair to warn you that you'd be wasting your time with Tom. He's a player.'

'Why do you think I'm gay?'

'You . . . you were asking about Tom, er, saying how handsome he is, asking if he's with anyone.'

JJ laughed out loud. 'Jess, I'm not gay. I was asking about Tom because . . . oh look there's Tanisha.' He broke off from what he was saying and waved.

I glanced up. 'Oh. My. God,' I blurted.

A vision had materialised at the other end of the spa. A dark-skinned goddess in a gold silk robe, her black hair tied up in a knot. It felt like someone had turned the lighting up a few notches as she looked over to us and waved.

'You know her?'

JJ nodded. 'Sure. She's an old friend of my mom's. In fact, she was over last night. Want to meet her?'

'D'er.' I didn't care that I was openly star-struck. I couldn't help it.

A few seconds later, she was standing in front of

us, her smile showing perfect whiter than white teeth. *Must use the same dentist as the Lewis family*, I thought. They all have super-white teeth as well.

'Hey, JJ,' she said in a soft American accent. 'And who's this?'

'Jess,' JJ replied. 'Jess is Mr Hall's daughter, you know, the general manager.'

She smiled. 'Oh sure. Hey, Jess, pleased to meet you. You all been swimming?'

I nodded. Once again, my brain seemed to have got up and gone. It was probably snoozing on a lounger on the other side of the spa. *Get back here, brain*, I told myself.

'How old are you, Jess?'

I couldn't remember. *How old am I?* I asked myself. 'Oh! Fifteen.'

She smiled. 'Interesting. Hey, JJ. Did you tell Jess about the competition?'

JJ shook his head. 'No.'

'What competition?' I asked.

'Tanisha's going to mentor a modelling competition in the next month,' JJ explained.

'Wow,' I said. Maybe she was going to give me tickets. 'How fab.'

'I hope so,' said Tanisha.

'Are you going to be in it?'

'Me? No. It's not for me. It's for teenagers. Say, Jess, how tall are you?'

'Five foot nine.'

'You ever thought about modelling?'

I burst out laughing. 'Yeah, right.'

'You're the right height, right age. Check out the website if you're interested. Teen model. A good-looking girl like you could go a long way.'

'B . . . but,' I stuttered. 'Me?' I'd never looked worse. Wet hair. No make-up. She couldn't be serious. Models had perfect skin, perfect hair, perfect bodies.

'Yeah, you.' She gave me a big smile. 'I'm on the hunt! Now I'm going to go and take me a swim. See you later.'

She sashayed off, dropped her robe to reveal a white bikini and a perfectly toned body. *Magazines pay thousands for what I'm looking at*, I thought as she dived into the water, and moments later, was cutting a perfect crawl through the water.

JJ grinned. 'Teen model hey? You going to go for it?'

'Oh yeah and I'm going to go in for *The X Factor*, *Junior Apprentice* and *MasterChef* too,' I said. I couldn't take it in. I had just met Tanisha and she had suggested that I go in for a modelling competition. It was unreal. I had to be dreaming.

Dream or not, I got no sleep that night. I kept replaying my conversation with JJ. Over and over. And over. *But you're gay?* I'd said those words to him but hadn't he denied it just before Tanisha came in? I can't remember. It all went blurry. Alisha came to join us and an older man from the apartments came to swim so I didn't hang around. *You're gay? But you're gay? I had said that and he'd laughed. Why had he laughed? Shut up, mind, shut up, I need to go to sleep. But you're gay. No mistaking. I had said it. What if he isn't? I'll have blown any chance I had with him forever. Ohhhhhhhhh God . . . And then I'd met Tanisha when I was looking my worst. She must have been being kind saying I should enter the competition, polite like the Lewises are. No way would anyone ever mistake me for a potential model. A huge spot on my chin. Wet hair. Oh God, oh Go-od. What had I said to her? Who me? Yeah, right. I should have said something more interesting. To both of them. But you're gay? You're gay? What must JJ think of me? If he's not gay, will he still like me? Does he like me? Is that why he wanted to hang out after swimming? Or was he checking out the situ with Tom? And what if*

Alexei's the one, not JJ or Tom? Oh arghhh. Actually Pia said Alexei is graceful. Maybe he's the gay one. Oh shut up, shut up, Jess. Boys can be graceful and not gay. Go to sleep. Count sheep. One two three. Oh no, the sheep are turning into boys, JJ, Alexei, Tom dressed in ballet tutus. Very camp. Wearing lipstick. But gays aren't always camp. Even I know that. So who's gay? How can you really tell? Oh God. I've gone mad.

Charlie popped his head around my bedroom door around midnight. 'I can hear you groaning,' he said. 'You OK?'

'No, I'm not. I am an idiot. The most stupid person in the whole world.'

'No change there then,' said Charlie as he shut the door and went back to bed.

Yeah, no change there, I thought as my mind went back to playing its loop tape.

4

Miss Teen

'I think we should all go for it,' I said as the girls and I sat in a cluster around my computer after school on Thursday. Pia, Flo, Meg and Alisha. We'd found the competition website by Googling Tanisha teen model UK.

Catwalk Teen Queen, it said on the home page.

Could that be you? Pop diva Tanisha will be sponsoring a modelling competition in London. Open to girls between fourteen and sixteen. Four rounds on four consecutive

Saturdays. If you think you've got what it
takes, get out that lipgloss and pencil the
dates in your diary NOW.

'The first date's in a fortnight,' said Flo.

'Wow, that's soon,' I said.

'Pia and I are too small,' said Meg as she tucked
into a muffin with honey.

'Says who?' I asked.

She pointed at the screen. 'Says them. See, in the
small print at the bottom. It says contestants need to
be five foot eight or over.'

'That's mad. OK so you might both be small but
you're gorgeous.'

'But we're midgets,' said Meg.

'Vertically challenged,' corrected Pia.

Meg didn't laugh. She doesn't like being small.
'Whatever. No-one wants to see Mini Mes on the
catwalk.'

'Rubbish,' I said. 'Kylie's only four foot something.
Smaller than you and so is her sister Dannii. Being
small never held them back and it shouldn't hold you
back either.'

'Yeah, but although Kylie and Dannii do a bit of
modelling, they're not *catwalk* models. You have to

be tall for the catwalk,' said Meg. 'You have to be the perfect clothes horse, which is tall and skinny.'

Pia shrugged. 'I appreciate what you're saying, Jess, but it's cool – being a model for the catwalk or magazines is not really my thing. You have to wear what other people tell you, cut and colour your hair the way they say. I prefer to make my own choices.'

I glanced back at the screen. 'Still, it's unfair. It leaves out a huge percentage of girls.'

'Fact. Clothes hang better on tall girls,' said Pia. 'Tall and skinny, that's what they want.'

'But most girls aren't tall and skinny. Take our class, for example – there are tall, short, fat, thin, all sorts. It's wrong to exclude anyone because they don't fit the model mould. I hate all that stuff. It just makes some people feel like losers, which is ridiculous.'

'What about you, Flo?' Meg asked. 'You going to go for it?' Flo was as tall as me with long blonde hair, flawless skin and big, grey, dreamy eyes. Every inch model material.

'Yeah maybe. What do you think, Jess?'

'I'm not doing it,' I said. 'I wouldn't get far anyway and I don't like that it's not open to everyone.'

'Oo, get you, Miss Political,' said Pia.

'I'm not entering if you're not,' said Flo. 'And anyway, you have to send in photos and I haven't got any. And you have to put down all sorts of stuff on the application,' she read from the screen, 'your hobbies, goals, what are you passionate about. How do you get on with your family?

I went to the application and typed:

Name: Princess Tallulah Fartnose-Smythe.
Height: three foot two.
Weight: fat with size extra extra large basoomas and very skinny legs and two heads.
Reaason why you want to model: So I can take over the world and also because I want to see people with two heads represented.
How do I get on with my family: Not well. They gave me indigestion when I ate them for lunch last Sunday.
Hobbies: naked wobbly dancing.
Passionate about: cake and naked wobbly dancing.

'What is naked wobbly dancing, Jess?' asked Flo.

'Obvious, dummy. Dancing naked—'

'And wobbling,' Pia finished for me and we all cracked up laughing.

'Shame we couldn't really put in a false application, just for a laugh,' said Pia. 'Listen. Print a couple of forms out and I'll get mad photos to go with them.'

'Send in a pic of me,' said Meg. 'I have short legs and a big bum.'

'Rubbish. Your bum's perfect,' I said.

Meg shook her head. 'It's out of proportion with the rest of me.'

'I have a boy's body,' said Alisha with a sigh.

'Give it back to him then,' I said.

'No, dummy,' Alisha persisted. 'I have no waist.'

'Me too,' said Flo. 'And my thighs are heavy.'

'I hate my feet,' said Pia. 'Like I'm small everywhere but then you see my feet. Ergh!'

Not to be left out, I added, 'I hate my nose. It's huge.'

'It so isn't,' said Pia.

'Seems no-one's happy with what they've got,' said Alisha.

'No,' we all chorused then sighed.

'What about you, Alisha?' asked Flo. 'You're tall enough. Will you go in for the competition?'

She shook her head. 'Mom and Dad would never

allow it otherwise I might have done. Be fun. But it's a non-starter. The press would be all over it. You can imagine, Jefferson Lewis's daughter in model competition; Tanisha, old friend of Mrs Lewis; a fix? Yada yada. And anyhow, we're back in LA in March because Dad's doing some scenes over there. So no go for me.'

'When will you be back?' I asked.

'We're only going for the month,' she replied. 'Then back here for a while.'

'Print me out some forms for fun,' said Pia. 'For Miss Ugly Bugly and her wobbly friends.' I did as she asked, printed out a couple, gave them to her then closed down the site. I felt relieved. I'd have felt weird about going in for the competition without my mates. I also wondered what people at school might have thought if I had gone in for it – like, would they have thought that I was so full of myself, and that I thought I was oh so pretty? I was glad I wouldn't have to deal with any of that stuff. No, having a laugh with my mates and groaning about what we didn't like about ourselves was much more fun.

I went to the loo to reapply my lipgloss. Alexei was expected any minute and I wanted to look my best. I still felt conflicted about liking him and JJ but it was still early days with both of them and my horoscope this morning had said that time would reveal the answer to a burning question. I took that question to be about my love life. When I came back into the room, I could tell by the silence that the girls had been talking about me.

'OK. What?'

Pia had been back on my computer and looked in my photo album. She'd pulled one that had been taken last summer onto the desktop. It was a rare shot of me looking OK for once. Charlie had taken it and I was smiling into the camera, and the sunlight had caught my hair, making it look shiny.

'We think you should enter,' said Meg. 'You're very photogenic.'

'No, we decided not. Just leave it.'

'Could be a way to earn some dosh,' said Pia. 'The prize is money and a spread in a mag. It would help boost your confidence. Help you see what a babe you are.'

The others nodded.

'I will if you will,' said Flo.

'You have to go for it. For the rest of us,' said Meg. 'When one of you wins, you can take us out on a great girlie shopping day.'

'No way I'd win. Absolutely no way,' I said. 'It would be a waste of time.'

Saved by the bell, I thought as the doorbell rang. I felt my stomach constrict. 'Oh. That will be Alexei. I don't want him up here in my bedroom. Come on, let's all go to the VIP shed.' The VIP shed is our den at the back of the garden. It was used for storage until Dad said Charlie and I could use it to hang out in. It's fab in there, with old rugs, a battered old sofa, cushions on the floor and a heater to keep us warm.

Flo went off to the loo and the others followed me down as I went to answer the door. Alexei stood there looking every bit as gorgeous as I had remembered him. He was carrying a stunning bunch of white flowers.

'Gardenias,' he said as he handed them to me, then produced a box of beautifully wrapped chocolates. I smiled but inwardly I sighed. It was lovely getting the gifts that he, and Alisha and JJ, brought when they came over but the bar of Cadbury's fruit and nut and potted daffodil that I could afford just didn't seem like an adequate return to their elegant designer presents.

'Thank you so much,' I said as I ushered him inside. He made a slight bow and stepped into our open-plan kitchen living room.

'Probably a bit smaller than your place,' I said as Pia

45

and Meg straightened up and smiled. Alisha nodded hi to him. She'd already met him when his family went to meet hers. Like Pia, she'd also dismissed him as 'not her type'. I introduced him to Meg and Pia, and as they were chatting, Flo appeared at the top of the stairs.

It was like watching a movie go into slow motion.

'And this is Flo,' I said.

He looked up at her as she descended the stairs. His eyes widened. She noticed him and her cheeks flushed pink. She lowered her eyelashes, looked back up at him and their eyes locked.

Now that's chemistry, I thought as Pia glanced over at me with sympathy. She'd seen it too, and for a few moments, it was like the rest of us didn't exist.

5

Pia's Project

Pia sent me a text the next morning.

Be at Alisha's Saturday 10am on pain of death.

'What are you up to?' I asked when we got the bus home from school on Friday. Every time I'd seen her in breaks, she'd been on her phone, texting or talking.

'All will be revealed tomorrow,' she said and went back to her texting. I tried to see over her shoulder but she put her hand over her phone. I looked out the window into the gloomy grey afternoon and thought about last night. We'd had a fun time in the VIP shed. Alexei seemed genuinely thrilled to meet us all and when Charlie and Henry came to join us, they all hit it off and talked music and movies. Anyone could see though, that despite the fact that we were in a group, Alexei and Flo only had eyes for each other, and I noticed that before he left, he took her number and email address. I couldn't help but feel a bit jealous even though I was glad for Flo. Like me, she'd never had a proper boyfriend, and it would boost her confidence to have had someone like Alexei so obviously smitten at first sight. I'd love it if a boy fell for me like that but it never seemed to happen that way. Maybe I just wasn't the type boys fell head over heels over. *So that leaves Meg, Alisha and me sans boyfriend*, I thought. 'All by my-se-e-elf,' I warbled.

Pia looked at me. 'And stop singing that song,' she said. 'That's if you can call what you do singing.'

'It's my theme song,' I replied. 'I am destined to be all alone forever.' I put on my best tragic heroine look, which is noble with a touch of sadness.

Pia laughed. 'And now you look like you've just sucked a lemon. You're such a drama queen. Mr Right will come along one of these days.'

'Yeah. He'll come along and walk right past me and into the arms of one of my mates.'

'Flo?'

I nodded.

'They make a nice couple. And honestly, Jess, I don't think he was the one for you and I think you knew it. You like guys with a bit of edge, like Tom, he's wicked, and anyone can see JJ's really bright. He knows about all sorts of stuff and that would keep you interested. Alexei seems . . . sweet, a romantic like Flo. I just can't see you liking someone gazing into your eyes like a big soppy dog. You'd have got bored and be longing for someone to give you a bit of cheek.'

'I wouldn't mind. I might like the chance to get bored with a boy and I can do romantic. I'm sure I could. You might be right though. I didn't feel a spark with Alexei and it was obviously there with him and Flo.'

Pia linked my arm. 'When you fall in love, it's going to be MAGnificent!'

'Yeah, right. Whatever.'

'When you meet the right one, it will be the love story to end all love stories. They will make movies out of it. It will be legend. You will be the modern Romeo and Juliet, Tarzan and Jane, er . . . Shrek and Princess Fiona. You will go together like the sun and the moon, er . . . bangers and mash, fish and chips.'

'You can shut up now, Pia.'

'OK,' she said and went back to her texting.

I went up to Alisha's the next morning at the allotted time. Pia opened the door. She was wearing all black, even a black beret on the side of her head.

'Very French,' I said as I stepped inside.

'Very photographer's assistant actually. Everyone's waiting for you in the living room.'

'Everyone?'

'Oui oui, my dahlink droopy drawers. I am Pia, la greatest stylist in la vorld. And I have not vasted ze time getting things organised. Now, come, come.'

'Are you doing a French or a Russian accent?'

'Cheek. Both,' said Pia. 'I like to embrace all ze nations. Anyway, come in. I have les assistants waiting to shoot.'

'Assistants? Shoot?' I asked. I so hoped that she wasn't harping on about the modelling competition. I wasn't in the mood. I couldn't help it but I was feeling totally unenthusiastic about that and everything. I was fifteen, never had had a proper relationship and it was getting me down. I so wanted a boyfriend and not to be constantly on an emotional roller-coaster, not knowing where I stood or how to be, saying the wrong thing then up half the night worrying about it like I had after I'd asked JJ if he was gay. 'I'm sorry, Pia, just I'm feeling low today. I'm beginning to feel that no-one will ever want to go out with me. Maybe I'm not boyfriend material. Maybe my destiny lies elsewhere. Maybe I am supposed to be a nun and that is what life is trying to tell me so if you're still on about the modelling competition, you can drop it now. It's not going to happen.'

Pia yawned. 'Blah blah blah blah blah.'

'So much for the sympathy. You're supposed to be my mate.'

'I am but you do go on sometimes, like a CD that's got stuck. You have to move on, baby.'

I felt like I was going to cry. *Must be my period*, I thought. *PMT, periods, post-periods. It's hard being a girl and a slave to hormones sometimes*. Pia could usually talk me out of any mood but this morning, I was feeling like a wet wimp. I turned to leave but Pia got that I was genuinely down. She caught my arm. 'Life is not telling you to shut yourself away and give up. Life is telling you to stop being so miserable and to listen to your friend Pia who is wiser than you,' she replied. 'Seriously, Jess, I want this modelling thing to happen for you. I knew that you'd take the fact that

Alexei fancies Flo personally, like a rejection but it wasn't like that. You saw what happened and it will happen for you one day.' She began to sing or rather warble. 'Soooome day your pri-in-ince will come.'

'Now who's like a CD that got stuck?' I put my fingers in my ears. 'If I agree to do a few shots, will you stop singing?'

Pia laughed. 'If that's what it takes. Yes. See, I'm not going to let you get into a downer about yourself so you're going to enter the competition and see for once and for all what a gorgeous babe you are.'

I went cross-eyed and stuck my tongue out.

'And you'll go a long way with a look like that,' said Pia.

I sighed. It was no use. She could be a right bossy-boots some days. She opened the door to the living room and there was the whole gang: Alisha, JJ, Meg, Flo, Henry, Charlie, even Alexei. It looked like they'd been there a while by the look of the table in front of them and the remnants of a breakfast of croissants, honey and jam.

'So you're in on this too?' I asked Charlie when he gave me a cheeky grin. 'What's going on?'

'We've been planning today's shoot,' said Flo.

'Shoot?'

Alisha came forward, linked my arm and pulled me towards the door. 'Today, you and Flo are our super-models and we are—'

'Your slaves,' said Henry and he got up and bowed. Like Pia, he was also dressed in black. He'd even pencilled in a black moustache with curly ends.

'But—' I objected. Seeing them all draped together on the sofa, they were the ones who looked like models from a magazine. They looked so relaxed with each other. Henry with his dark brooding looks; Alexei next to him, blond and beautiful and totally at home despite the fact he'd only just met everyone; Charlie, tall with his fine features and floppy hair. Meg sweet and blonde; Flo tall and dreamy-eyed; JJ tall, classically handsome; and Alisha with her glossy shoulder-length hair and perfect figure.

'Come on, Jess,' said Pia. 'Flo's up for it. It will be fun. Henry's going to take the pics, JJ's going to do the lighting, Alexei is going to art direct and as Alisha is roughly the same height, she's going to style and has very kindly offered to lend her clothes.'

'I've already picked out a few looks,' Alisha said. 'They're laid out on the bed upstairs.'

'I'm going to do make-up,' said Meg. 'And JJ's going to take orders for refreshments and be our runner.'

'Yep, I'm all yours,' said JJ and he gave me a look that made my toes curl. I immediately felt myself beginning to perk up.

'Come on, Jess,' said Alisha. 'Mum and Dad are gone for the day. I've always wanted to be a stylist and this place gets great light even at this time of year.'

I had to admit the Lewises' apartment was the perfect location to do a photo shoot. It looked just like an interior from a glossy design magazine and the neutral shades of earth and stone that Mrs Lewis had chosen gave an air that was elegant and expensive.

'And I'm going to provide some perfect background music to get you in the mood,' said Charlie and he began to strum on his guitar.

I looked around. Everyone was focused on me. I couldn't cop out now. Plus a chance to try on some of Alisha's clothes was very tempting. Her wardrobe was awesome. 'OK. OK but—'

'No buts,' said Pia and she clapped her hands. 'Hair and make-up, take Jess and Flo upstairs.'

I followed them up to Alisha's dressing room where they'd laid out make-up on her dressing table. Pia and Meg soon got busy applying gloss and a little shadow for a natural look and Alisha fussed around bringing out accessories. The rest of the morning flew by. We started with casual shots in the living room and out on the terrace with the park behind us. Luckily it was a bright cloudless day so we didn't freeze to death out there. The boys were careful to use different backgrounds for Flo and me so that it didn't look as if we were in the same place. No problem with that as the apartment is vast. For the outside shots, Alisha produced an amazing selection of sunglasses to try: Prada, Chanel, Gucci, seemed she had a pair by every designer there was. I chose a dark brown pair by Armani. I kept my jeans on, Meg gave me a pale green T-shirt and Alisha added a fab leather belt and a pair of high-heeled brown suede Manolo Blahnik boots just like the ones I'd seen Beyonce wearing on TV. I was in fashion heaven.

'OK. Jess, put your shoulders back, chin down, head a little this way,' Henry instructed from behind the video camera as I draped myself over a life-size Balinese statue in the hall. 'Give me a nice pout. That's it. Pretend you're a star.'

'You *are* a star,' said Alisha. 'Now act like one. You're already a model and you're playing a part. You're a supermodel who only gets out of bed for a million a day. You got it, so flaunt it.'

I did as I was instructed and flaunted, strutted and posed like a professional – or at least my idea of one. It was fun being the centre of attention and my runner, JJ, got me what I wanted while all around, the others also got into their role as part of the supermodel team.

After a short break for lunch, JJ suggested that we did swimwear.

'We could do the shots around the infinity pool out on the terrace,' he said.

'But it will be cold in just our cossies,' Flo objected.

'The water's as warm as in the Caribbean,' said Alisha. 'There's underfloor heating under the tiles around the pool, the water's body temperature, even the loungers are heated. You'll be warm as toast out there.'

Once again, I was reminded why the apartments cost millions. It wasn't just the spectacular views over Hyde Park or the location in the heart of Knightsbridge, it was all the hidden extras that delivered a luxurious lifestyle: summer swimming in winter, perfect climate control in every room, subtle lighting in the evening, sound systems in every room operated by the flick of a hidden switch. Everything designed for maximum comfort.

For the pool shots, I chose a turquoise bikini and Flo a red one. Alisha gave us silk sarongs to match. Meg pulled our hair back, and applied bright red lipstick. I wore big black Chanel glasses, Flo a tres chic Gucci pair.

Alisha sprayed us with some French perfume I'd never heard of. 24 Faubourg. It smelt exquisite. 'To really get in the mood,' she said as she sprayed it over Meg and Pia too.

At last JJ can see me looking more glam, I thought as we wafted out to the pool area. JJ and Henry were already out there. Every time I glanced over at JJ, he was watching me. My earlier mood had disappeared completely. It felt great.

'I feel like I'm on holiday in some exotic location,' I said as I lay back on the heated lounger and Alexei handed me a pink drink in a cocktail glass to use as a prop.

'They help,' said Flo. She pointed to the six perfectly potted palm trees lining the top of the pool. 'Coconut anyone?'

The evening party dress shots were the best fun. Alisha let us choose our own dresses from her collection. Her wardrobe is the size of a double bedroom and is wall to wall full of colour co-ordinated clothes and shoe racks, with a floor-to-ceiling mirror at one end. We were spoilt for choice. There were designers I knew but many American ones who were new to me. *This isn't like we're doing it for a competition*, I thought, *it feels like the dressing-up games I've played with Pia since we were little.*

'Try whatever you like,' said Alisha with a grin. 'Try looks that you wouldn't normally as some things look better on than on the hanger.' She grabbed an armful and threw them over a chair.

In the end, we tried on just about everything and Meg and Pia couldn't resist and tried things on too even though they were way too long for them. Not to be left out, Alisha joined in as well.

'I'd forgotten I had this,' she said as she picked out a white chiffon party dress which looked like the perfect prom dress.

'And Alexei seems to be having a good time,' said Pia as she handed me a Versace gold silk dress to try. 'He fits right in.'

I nodded. 'Has he asked you out yet, Flo?'

'He asked me to see a movie tonight,' she said with a shy smile.

'Where are you going to go? Odeon?' I asked.

'There's a home cinema in his apartment,' she said

as she slipped into a halter-neck long pale blue dress. 'Cool, huh?'

The dress looked divine. Floaty was so Flo's style.

Of course, I thought as Alisha began to make up my eyes in smokey greys. A home cinema. Alexei, JJ and Alisha might be the same age as us but their lifestyles were on another planet with their home cinemas, private heated pools and chauffeured limos. Even something as simple as a glass of juice was hand-squeezed to order by the housekeeper and probably made from fruits flown in that morning from the other side of the world. Today though, it didn't seem to matter that my background was poorer. We were just a bunch of teens hanging out having a super-brilliant time.

In the end, I settled for a Stella McCartney short royal blue dress which fitted me perfectly and Flo went for the pale blue one, and our make-up girls finished their magic.

'You look stunning,' said Flo when we were ready.

'And so do you,' I said. I felt amazing, a million dollars, which I was probably wearing when Alisha added a silver necklace and charm bracelet and dove grey Jimmy Choo strappy heels.

'The party dress shots are going to be in the hall

for you, Flo. I want you to act as if you've just arrived and you're saying hi to a bunch of guests,' said Henry when we went down. Alexei couldn't take his eyes off her and she smiled back at him. Pia had been right. They would look great together. 'And Jess, I want you to stand at the bar in the kitchen, look to your side as if you've just seen someone come in that you fancy. Mouth closed, show it in your eyes. OK, I'll start with you, Jess. I'll start in close-up on you, best pouty look, then I'll pan across to Flo.'

I had to laugh. Henry was in his element.

We took our places while Henry and JJ fiddled with the lights. Alexei got busy in the kitchen, dressing the room with glasses and bottles so it looked like a party.

'See how JJ's looking at you,' whispered Pia as I took my place at the bar. 'That boy is into you big time.

I glanced over at him. He met my eyes. He didn't smile. His look was intense and I felt it right down in the pit of my tummy.

'You look lovely, Jess,' he said.

I indicated the four-inch heels I was wearing. 'Thanks. I just hope I can keep standing and not fall over. Model splattered on the floor is probably not the look they're after.'

'OK, action,' called Henry. He'd told me to look up

as if someone I fancied had just walked in. I looked over at JJ. He was still watching me.

'Great,' said Henry. 'That's the look!'

I laughed and JJ's eyes twinkled. The day was getting better and better.

After my shots, I went to watch Flo. She did her entrance then Alexei asked her to go into the living room and lie back on the sofa. She did as she was told and Alexei placed a cushion behind her then directed her to fling her arm behind her head. I glanced over at Pia and smiled. Alexei looked as if he'd like to jump on top of Flo. Pia smiled back. She knew what I was thinking – that major love chemistry was happening in this place today. I glanced over at the others. I hoped that Meg, Alisha and Charlie didn't feel left out.

'Oh, get a room,' said Pia as Alexei arranged Flo's hair out in a fan on the cushion behind her. JJ caught my eye as everyone laughed and it felt as if we were sharing a private joke.

Flo looked so happy and I felt glad for her. I couldn't be jealous, especially not after the way that JJ had been looking at me all day. I wondered how Charlie was feeling seeing Flo and Alexei together. Flo'd liked Charlie for ages but he always made out that he wasn't interested in girls and that had knocked her confidence. It was great to see her getting the attention she deserved. I glanced over at Charlie who was watching the scene along with the rest of us. He had a hard look on his face. I knew that look. It was one he put on when he didn't want anyone to know what he was feeling. Maybe he wasn't as disinterested as he'd appeared.

When we were done, Henry, Charlie and Pia went off to edit, Alexei took Meg and Flo up to his apartment and I was left alone with Alisha and JJ.

Alisha soon made herself scarce. 'Er . . . think I'll go and do some emails,' she said and headed for her room.

JJ opened the tall glass door to the terrace and beckoned me to follow him out onto there. 'You looked great today,' he said.

I leant up against the wall. 'Thank you.'

'And Jess . . . about the other day?'

'Oh, yes, er . . . I—'

'About me being gay?'

'Oh that, yes, I—' I was about to apologise. I had a whole speech planned but before I could start, JJ stepped towards me, slipped one hand around my waist and pulled me to him. With his other hand, he stroked my cheek and looked into my eyes. Wuhoo! Gulp. I felt a rush, sweet and intense, go through me. He leant forward and brushed my lips gently with his. He pulled back to check my reaction then leant forward again and kissed me, this time, not so gently.

Alisha had been right earlier. It was toasty warm out on the terrace.

6

Kudos

'The dance. Alisha was so right,' I said to Pia in break at school a few days later. 'Show you're interested in a boy and he steps back, act like you're disinterested and he steps forward.'

I hadn't been acting either. Since JJ had kissed me, I hadn't even thought about Tom. I'd seen him about school but was so not interested. He could play his games, I didn't care. I had someone who liked me and wasn't messing me around and he'd promised that when he was back from LA at the end of March, he'd like to take me out. It felt so nice to have a boy be straight, not be all maybe I'm into you, maybe not like Tom, like he was keeping his options open in case he got a better offer. JJ just came out with it – Jess, I'm into you. It felt great. However, I hesitated about telling him how much I liked him too in case he thought I was a pushover. I kept reminding myself that boys like a challenge. He'd sent me a text the day after the photo shoot saying how much he'd enjoyed it and instead of replying straight away, I'd waited twenty-four hours then wrote back, ditto. Cool. Casual. That was me. Curiously though, my new indifference seemed to be having an effect on Tom and on Friday night after school, he was waiting outside by the bus stop for me. He was looking very cute with his leather jacket turned up against the cold, a long grey scarf wrapped around his neck, and his hair which was slightly wet from the damp air was slicked back from his face.

'Hey, Hall. Have you heard from the modelling competition yet?' he asked.

I shook my head. 'Ah, so you heard about that?'

He nodded. It wasn't surprising. It had soon got round school that Flo and I had entered. The competition was the talk of every break and lunchtime: who'd gone in for it – quite a few from our school apparently. Who the favourites were. All the entrants said that it was for fun. We were all being so cool about it, like, no, we hadn't heard. Hahaha, what a laugh. I got the feeling, though, that there was a part in all of us that secretly hoped, laugh or not, that we might get through. There's certainly a part of me that does. No denying. Last Saturday had been fun, fun, fun, and it was obvious that it had given Flo and I kudos at school, like we were just that bit more interesting than we were previously.

Tom moved closer and I caught his scent. He always smelt good, the leather of his jacket mixed with something clean and woody. 'Yes. I like the idea of dating a model.'

'Is that right? That's assuming I'd go on a date with you.'

Tom's eyes twinkled with mischief and as he moved in even closer, I felt a tingle of electricity. 'And that's assuming that I was referring to you.'

I decided I'd play him at his own game. 'Of course you were. You know you can't resist me, Robertson. Just admit it then accept that I am out of your league and move on.'

He cracked up, then stood back and looked right into my eyes. I wished he wouldn't do that. It always had the same effect and right on cue, my stomach lurched pleasantly and I blushed. *JJ*, I told myself.

Forget Tom. He's playing. He only responds to a challenge, and will always do my head in. I took a step back and looked away as if I was getting bored.

'Ah Hall, you heartbreaker you,' he said and he put his hands to his heart. 'Seriously though, have you heard yet?'

'No. Soon. We got an automated reply saying entrants would hear by the end of next week. I won't get through. There are thousands of people going in for it. Flo and I are doing it for a laugh really.'

He put his arm around me. 'Don't be too modest. You got the height, the looks. You scrub up well.'

'Scrub up well? Thanks a bunch.'

'Charlie told me all about your session up chez Lewis. I saw some of the footage on his laptop when we got together for band practice. You looked hot. You should have let me know. I could have helped too.'

I was never sure with Tom what his motives were and whether he wanted to come over to be with me or to hang out with me so he could see inside Porchester Park and get in with the richies.

'Thanks. Actually we had a good team.'

'I heard. I saw,' said Tom. 'And it sounds like I might have some competition. JJ, Alexei.' He pulled a sad face and pushed out his bottom lip.

'Yeah, like you care, Tom Robertson.'

'But I do, Hall. You're one of my favourite girls.'

'Exactly, *one* of your favourites. Not your favourite.'

'Ah. Now that wouldn't be fair on all the others, would it? Imagine the hurt that would cause. The broken hearts. No. I have a duty to keep as many as possible happy.'

I laughed. 'You're so arrogant. And you know what? The way you are, you don't make anyone happy.'

Tom scrutinised me. 'Are you saying I've made you unhappy?' He looked pleased and I realised I'd given away too much. I didn't want him to know just how much he'd affected me. I flicked my hair over my shoulder and gave him a disdainful look. 'You? As if. I just feel sorry for the suckers on your list.'

Tom pretended to swoon. 'You charmer you. Seriously though, you know you have my heart.'

'Yeah. I keep it pickled in a jar in the fridge, behind the cheese and eggs.'

Tom cracked up again. It was so weird. Now I felt cooler towards him, I could crack jokes. When I felt I wanted something from him, my brain turned to sludge.

The dance. Yep. Back and forward we go, I thought as my bus appeared on the horizon. 'Ciao,' I said to

Tom as I stuck my hand out for the bus to stop. 'Have fun breaking hearts.'

The next morning, I went to meet Keira. She'd sent me a message on Facebook asking to meet at eleven at a café near her house. Then a second message changing the time to ten forty-five.

I arrived five minutes early. Ten forty-five came and went. Eleven. Eleven fifteen. I didn't have her mobile number, nor did she have mine, so I decided to give her another quarter of an hour. I got out my jotter and doodled Tom's name. I realised what I'd done so doodled JJ's. I was about to leave when the café door opened and in Keira came, all smiles and a big wave. She sat opposite me, no apology, no explanation. She looked at my cup.

'You had a drink already?'

I wanted to say, yeah, course I have, I've been here for ages and you're forty-five minutes late, but I didn't. I nodded. 'Yes. Latte.'

'Are you going to have another?'

'Oh. Er . . . Maybe.'

'Great. Can you get me something when you go to the counter? I just got to make an urgent call. I'd like a hot chocolate. Large one. Thanks. And can you get

69

me a sandwich? Cheese and tomato. I'm starving. I'll pay you back. Is that OK?'

'Pay me back?'

'Yeah. I left my money at home, I was in such a rush to get here. Hey, it's not a problem, is it?'

I felt mean. 'No. Course not.' I checked my purse. I had just enough left of my pocket money.

'Don't look so worried, Jess. I'll pay you back next time I see you. Promise. Unless you want interest on it that is.' She laughed at her own joke but I didn't find it funny. She'd managed to make me feel mean and distrusting and all in a couple of sentences. *I'm going to get her sandwich, drink my drink, then I'm out of here and I don't think I want to hang out with her even if she is just here for a month or so,* I thought as I stood in the queue and watched her take out her mobile, call someone and talk to them while keeping an eye on me. She said something, kept looking over at me and laughed. I was sure she'd said something cruel about me. *No-one else on the planet has this effect on me,* I thought. *I always feel wrong when I'm with Keira and I don't know if it's her or me. It's weird.*

I brought our drinks back to the table and noticed she'd been flicking through my jotter but she closed it quickly then tucked into the sandwich with relish.

'Thanks, you're a hon,' she said between mouthfuls. 'So what've you been doing, Jess? Swimming?' She said it in her usual mock tone. I decided that it was time to show her I'd moved on, grown up and wasn't the kid she used to be able to push around

'Actually, I've just entered a modelling competition,' I said as I spooned froth off my drink.

Her face registered a tiny flash of interest. 'What? Like at school?'

'No. It's open for any teenager in London, aged fourteen to sixteen.'

She stayed silent for a few moments as if thinking or not interested. 'So how did you hear about this competition?' she asked finally.

'Someone where I live is sponsoring it.'

'Like a girl-guide leader? Teacher?'

'No. Her name's Tanisha. You've probably heard of her.'

Keira scoffed. 'Oh course I've heard of *the* Tanisha. Pop star diva. So who's *your* Tanisha.'

I couldn't help it. I was enjoying having one over her for a change. 'Oh, she is *the* Tanisha.'

Keira scoffed again. 'Yeah right. As if. Like you'd live in the same place as her.'

I raised an eyebrow, ever so cool. 'My dad is general manager of a very upmarket apartment block in Knightsbridge and I mean, *very* upmarket.'

Keira looked at me like she wasn't sure if I was kidding. 'What's the competition called?'

'Catwalk Teen Queen.'

'I might Google it for a laugh when I get home. Open to anyone?'

'You have to be over five foot eight and between fourteen and sixteen. My mates wanted to go in for it but Pia and Meg—'

Keira laughed. 'Are too small.'

I suddenly realised that Keira wasn't too small. She was perfect model material. I felt a sinking feeling in my stomach. *I should have kept my big mouth shut,* I told myself. *Why oh why do I always have to blurt everything out or show off?*

'And were you going to let me know about it?'

'I just did,' I blurted but I felt bad again, like I'd been holding out on her, and actually, I wished I had. 'But I think you'll have missed the deadline.'

'Not my thing really,' she said and she looked at my hot chocolate. 'Better give up that if you're serious, my dear. Bad for the skin and you know what they say, a moment on the lips, a lifetime on the hips.

Luckily, I've never had to worry about my weight.' She glanced down at my stomach. *Insinuating that I do*, I thought.

'So how's your love life?' she asked.

No way was I going to tell her. 'Non-existent. Yours?' She half smiled. 'A work in progress.'

Oh God, don't let it be Tom, I thought as I remembered her standing watching my bus after she'd come to meet me at school. 'So you've met someone?'

'Early days.'

'From your school?'

Keira scoffed. 'As if. Too young. Don't you find? Schoolboys are so immature.'

'Yeah. Some.'

'But what about you? Anyone at your school you like?'

'Not really.'

'So who was the boy I saw blow you a kiss?'

So she had noticed him, I thought. *But she wouldn't be asking who he was if she'd met him that day.* 'Oh him. Just a guy who's full of himself, thinks every girl fancies him.'

Keira scrutinised my face. 'And do they?'

'Some.'

'Not you though.'

'As if,' I said. 'I don't like players. He's the kind that only likes a challenge then moves on.'

'Sounds like my kind of guy,' said Keira, then she leant over and ruffled my hair. 'Oh don't worry. I'm not going to trespass on your territory.'

'Not mi—' I was about to object but Keira's phoned bleeped that she had a text. She glanced down at it then got up to go. 'Later,' she said. 'Thanks for the sandwich and good luck with your beauty pageant.'

'It's not a pageant, it's a—' But she'd gone. I sighed. Once again, she'd managed to belittle what I was doing as well as leave me six pounds out of pocket. She'd brought up so many feelings and all in the space of an hour. I felt mean because I resented her asking to borrow money when I didn't have much to lend. Guilty because I felt mean about it. It was only a sandwich and a drink. Suspicious because I wondered if she was being honest about Tom. Angry because she'd been so late, like my time didn't matter but her time did. *Thank God for Pia, Meg, Flo and Alisha, my mates in a million*, I thought. *I never feel like this around them.*

7

Round One

The news came by email. No fanfare. No posh letter.
Just:

> Dear Jessica Hall,
> Congratulations.
> You've made it through to the first round of
> the competition. Out of 2000 entrants, fifty girls
> have been chosen. Please be at No 300–320,
> Atlas Buildings on Saturday . . .

The rest of the message was a blur as I reached for the
phone to call Pia.

'Unbelievable,' I said.

'No it isn't, it's totally believable. I told you you'd make it,' she said. 'Flo's through too. She just texted me. The boys did such a great job with your shots, the competition organisers couldn't have said no to either of you.'

I couldn't deny the thrill I felt. I was in. One of the chosen fifty! I read the rest of the letter then called Flo to compare notes. What were we going to wear? Where to meet? It felt unreal, as if my fairy godmother had appeared, waved her wand and declared, 'You shall go to the ball.'

All too soon, it was the big day and Flo and I met outside the tube station at Kensington High Street then went to find Atlas Buildings in a nearby side street where we joined the line of girls waiting to go in. Dad had insisted that Aunt Maddie accompany me and Flo's elder sister, Emma, came along with her. At first I thought I'd feel embarrassed to have a chaperone but it looked as if loads of girls had come with one of their parents or guardian. We were all well wrapped up because even though it was March and the sky was bright blue, it was bitterly cold, so cold that Emma and Aunt Maddie went off to the café opposite to get hot drinks. I was so pleased that

Flo was with me to chat to as the door opened and the group began to file in. I could see that everyone felt excited to be there, all of us eyeing each other up, wondering what was going to happen. Some girls looked very glamorous in high heels and loads of make-up. Flo and I had chosen to wear just a little shadow and lipgloss and both of us had decided to come dressed in our normal clothes so that we felt comfortable. Under our jackets, I was in my jeans and a coral-coloured jumper and Flo was wearing her jeans and a pale grey jumper with a pink scarf.

'Some of these girls are stunning,' Flo commented as we watched a tall blonde girl in front of us with cheekbones like cut glass brush her long silken hair. 'Oh God. I'm so nervous.'

'Me too. This isn't hanging out with mates and playing dressing up, this is for real.'

Flo nodded. 'Though it feels totally unreal.'

'Exactly,' I agreed. 'Henry made us look so fab in the photos he sent, I hope the judges won't be disappointed when they see me in the flesh. Maybe I should have dressed up more.'

'Maybe not. From what I've read about models, you have to show that you can do different looks according to what clothes you're wearing and what the modelling job is so it probably doesn't make that much difference what we turn up in today. We're supposed to be like blank canvases and the judges will be looking for versatile as well as photogenic.'

'I can juggle, tennis balls,' I said. 'Do you think that might show that I'm versatile and impress them? Show them I can do different things? Maybe I should show them I can lick my eyebrows?'

'Yeah, right,' said Flo. 'And I can do cartwheels and card tricks.'

Once inside, we gave our names at a desk, were given numbers then were put into groups of ten by a striking black lady with short hair who introduced herself as Suzie and who seemed to be in charge. Sadly Flo wasn't going to be in my group. As we waited to hear what was to happen next, I looked around at the other girls.

'Oh my God times two!' I said as I spotted Keira at the far end of the room. *What's she doing here?* I wondered. She looked amazing and even in the group of model wannabes, she stood out in a black romper suit, black leggings, black Ugg boots and bright red scarf.

'Who is it?' asked Flo as Keira waved and began to come over.

'Someone I used to know in junior school,' I said.

'Surprise,' said Keira and air-kissed me. 'Mwah, mwah.'

'Keira, hi,' I said and introduced her to Flo. 'What are you doing here?'

She looked as if I'd insulted her. 'What am I doing here? Excuse me? Same as you. I got through.'

'But the deadline?'

'Oh that? You know me. I blagged my way in – told them some story about my computer being down and they were cool with it. I don't give up when I've decided I want something.'

'Yes of course but . . . why didn't you message me?' I asked.

'Why didn't you message me?'

'I . . . Oh, I thought you said it wasn't your thing. I—'

Keira laughed and waved her hand as if dismissing that conversation. 'That was before I realised this was a big number. You weren't joking. *The* Tanisha no less! I looked the competition up online. Way to go, Jess.' She turned to Flo. 'She was holding out on me.'

'No I wasn't. I told you exactly what was happening.'

Keira laughed. 'Chill, Jess. Just teasing you.' She turned to Flo and talked to her as if I wasn't there. 'She's so easy to wind up, isn't she?'

Flo linked arms with me. 'But why would you want to do that?'

Keira ignored her comment and turned back to me. 'I thought you were kidding when you said you lived in the same place as Tanisha. I'd better come and check it out soon, least when you *finally* get round to inviting me that is.'

'I—' I didn't know what to say and couldn't think fast enough. I hadn't held out on her and she'd only been back in the country a short time and, come to think of it, she hadn't invited me to her house either! Not that I'd want to go. As always around Keira, I felt wrong-footed and uncomfortable.

Keira looked at me and laughed again. 'Your face, Jess. It was a picture when you saw me! Sorry I didn't let you know I'd entered but I didn't want to get you worried about being competition too early on.'

Suzie began to call the first group to go through and Keira heard her name.

'See you later, guys. May the best man win,' she said and went off to join her group.

'I wasn't holding out on her—' I started.

Flo squeezed my arm. 'Hey, you don't have to explain yourself to me. Anyway, I don't like her.'

'Why not?' I asked. It was very unusual for Flo

to dislike anyone. She usually saw the good side of everyone.

She shrugged. 'There was a girl like her at my junior school. A mean girl who always dissed everyone behind their back and even to their faces. Her only way to make herself feel better was to put everyone down. At first, people thought she was funny but after a while, it grated. She was always so negative. Keira's just like her, it was like she was trying to make you feel uncomfortable.'

'She does have that effect,' I said. 'I don't know what I feel when I'm with her. Odd, that's for sure.' Part of me wished I hadn't mentioned the competition to Keira but it was too late, she was in. *Never mind,* I told myself, *I probably won't get through after today then won't have to see her again.*

Flo's name was called next and she went off to join her ten. She pulled a face as she went. She didn't want to be separated either.

I sat on a bench and texted Aunt Maddie that we were fine and would meet her outside later. While I waited for my group to be called, I tried to get chatting with a pretty girl with short dark spiky hair.

'I won't get through,' I said. 'My nose is too big and I have a tummy.'

I thought she'd join in like my mates did when we had a down-on-ourselves conversation. She didn't. She gave me a disdainful look. 'Why did you enter if you don't think you've got what it takes?' she asked. 'Moaning about the way you look won't wash here. They want confidence.' She got up and moved away as if I was a bad smell. I listened in to a couple of other girls who were talking nearby.

'I don't know what some girls are even doing here,' said a blonde girl as she looked around at the contestants. 'I can't believe some of them got through.'

I glanced away. She probably meant me.

'Yeah. So many of them want to be chummy but I'm not here to make friends,' said her friend. 'It's business, not a social outing.'

I decided not to try and get talking to them and was relieved when my phone bleeped that I had two messages. Pia had texted: **Good luck gorgeous girl.** And Alisha had written. **It's all an act so act confident. A XXXXX**

As I sat there, I wondered what I'd let myself in for. Part of me wanted to do a runner but Flo would kill me if she came out and found I'd deserted her. After what felt like an endless long

wait, my group of ten were called into a confer-
ence room where there were two women and a man
sitting behind a long table. Suzie followed us in
and indicated we should stand in a line in front of
them. It felt really weird as we looked at the panel
and they stared back at us. The man looked about
sixty, friendly, with blue twinkly eyes, a white beard
and very short hair. He was wearing a black leather
jacket and looked like one of the arty crowd my
gran hangs out with. The woman next to him was
striking, smart in a tailored grey suit, bright red
lipstick, and she had her dark hair scraped back.
She looked scary in a Wizard of Oz, Wicked Witch
of the West kind of way and stared right through
me. The second lady had long blonde hair and big
brown eyes and she was dressed in layers of pale
green. She looked a bit scary too, she wasn't smiling like the man.

'OK, everyone. Quick introductions to your judges.
This is Derek Dawson,' said Suzie, 'some of you may
already know him and his work for *Vogue*, *Harper's*,
Tatler, all the glossies. We're very lucky to have him.
Next to him is Karie Mansfield, editor of *City Girl*
magazine, and on the right is Jackie Canning who
runs Model M. Most of you have already met me. I'm

Suzie Ashford. I'll be your co-ordinator today. Any questions or concerns, just come to me.'

We were asked to step forward one by one for a short interview.

'A chance to get to know the girl behind the photo,' Suzie explained.

As I listened to the first few girls, I realised that I was shaking inside. This wasn't a game any more. It wasn't the laugh I'd imagined, it was terrifying. A few girls sounded confident, a few not so sure, and one girl could hardly talk at all and Derek had to ask her to speak up. I tried to take in what they were saying in order to prepare myself but part of my brain seemed to have left the room.

'Jessica Hall,' called Suzie.

I put my hand up.

'Step forward,' said Suzie.

'Where are you from?' asked Derek.

'London,' I said.

'And why do you want to be a model, Jessica?' asked Jackie.

'I . . .' I had no idea. I didn't even know if I wanted to be a model but the people sitting in front of me didn't look like they'd appreciate it if I told them that and wouldn't like me wasting their time. They were waiting for me to say something. 'Act,' said Alisha's voice in my head. 'Pretend like you're already the best.' *Oh, God*, I thought, *this is my* X Factor *moment. Don't blow it, Jess.* I made myself stand tall. 'I've always loved clothes and the fashion world and I'd love to be an active part of it.'

Derek smiled and Karie nodded. *Phew*, I thought.

Jackie frowned. 'Modelling is hard work, Jessica. Long hours, all conditions. Do you think you have what it takes?'

'Oh yes,' I said. 'Absolutely.' *Oh no*, I thought. *And remind me to kill Pia when I get out of here. I will get through today then that's it. I don't want to be looked at the way the judges are and I don't want to compete with other girls. I thought this would be fun, but it so isn't.*

'Our winner has to have IT. You know what I mean by IT. What do you think IT is?' said Derek.

'Hard to define,' I said. 'But you know it when you see it.' I gave them a big smile.

They didn't look impressed and Jackie nodded to Suzie.

'OK, next,' she called. 'Emma Summers.'

I stepped back into the line and another girl stepped forward. I couldn't wait to get out but it wasn't over after our brief interview. We all trooped back into the main room and as we waited, girls used the time to reapply lipgloss, text or brush their hair. The atmosphere felt tense and no-one was chatting any more. The door opened and in a second, the mood in the room changed from anxious to excited. It was Tanisha. She peeled off her parka and dropped it on a chair. She was wearing a skin-tight jeans, a black T-shirt and high black boots. Even dressed in normal clothes, she exuded glamour.

'Hi, girls,' she said and gave us a wave.

'Hi,' we chorused back. I could see that my competitors were as star-struck as I was.

'Just checking in with y'all,' she said as she surveyed the room. When she spotted me, she gave me the tiniest wink in acknowledgement. I guess she didn't want to show any favouritism. Kiera leant forward, caught my eye and raised her eyebrow to let me know that although no-one else had seen Tanisha wink at me, she'd noticed.

'I don't know if Suzie's explained or not but after today,' Tanisha continued, 'twenty girls will go through to round two. I wish I could take you all but you know the score, there has to be eliminations. If you don't get through and you still want to make it in the modelling world, don't give up. It will be good preparation because you won't always get every job you go for and you can't take it personally or else you won't last a week. If you do get through, remember, be punctual. In the modelling world, time is money and if you're late for a photo shoot, it can cost thousands. So, good luck with it all and remember, every one of you is beautiful. Be kind with each other and remember, it's only a competition. OK, lecture over! I'm going to go say hi to the others, have a chat and see how you've all been getting on today. 'kay. Bye for now.'

'Byeee,' we chorused as she swept out of the room, and a buzz of chatter filled the room.

Suzie came through and clapped her hands for silence. 'Next we're going to give you a task. We're going to see if you can sell a product,' she said. 'I can see you've all got the looks – you wouldn't have got this far if you hadn't – but can you sell?' She indicated a camera to the left of the room which was surrounded by lights. I hadn't noticed it when I'd come in because I'd been too busy shaking and watching the other girls. 'A model has to be able to sell anything and today your job is to sell an organic drink that's new on the market. Each girl will have exactly one minute. Don't think about it too much, this is just to see if you can adapt in any situation and what each of you do. Be spontaneous.'

A few girls looked panicked but strangely I didn't feel too bad about having to do the task. We'd done things like this at school in drama when our teacher would give us a prop and ask us to improvise. I also felt more relaxed since I'd told myself that after today, I wasn't coming back. More than anything though, I was aware of my rumbling stomach. I was starving but neither Flo nor I had thought to bring anything to eat or drink and it didn't look as if anything was going to be provided.

The girl who could hardly talk in the first interview went on and fluffed it. She made no sense at all. I felt sorry for her because she was first and thrown in the deep end. A girl with spiky hair was second. She was amazing. She made a name up for the product, looked straight at the camera and seemed totally in control. Flo was OK but I could see that she was nervous and her voice was a bit flat. Keira was really good, smooth and confident, and I noticed Jackie turned to Karie and nod as though she liked what she saw.

Soon it was my turn. I took my place, took a deep breath, looked at the camera and just as I was about to speak, my stomach made a loud gurgle. 'I— woah! Oops.' I went bright red. A few girls tittered. I burst out laughing too because my stomach continued to grumble and growl. There was no stopping it, no matter how much I tried to breathe in and hold my stomach muscles. Gurgle, gurgle, it went. 'Yes, when hunger strikes, you know it's time for Gogo juice,' I said to camera. I remembered what our drama teacher always said in class about not being static and to move around to make an act more visual so I decided to do a jungle dance to go with my commercial for the juice. 'Ah rumble, ah rumble, rumble in the jungle with GOGOOO juice.' Gurgle wurgle, my stomach joined in.

Suzie and the cameraman looked at me as if I was mad. *And so ends my short but sweet career as a model,* I thought. I felt that there was nothing else to do except smile at the camera and bow.

8

Challenge

Later that evening, I was sitting with Pia, Charlie and Henry with my feet up in front of the telly. As a treat, Dad had let us get fish and chips.

'Yumbocious,' I said as I finished off my last chip.

'Indeedie doodie,' said Charlie. He threw a chip in the air and caught it in his mouth. He's a strange boy.

'Well, you gave it your best shot,' said Pia.

'I did. I honestly did but some of those girls were so serious, I mean, they had personal trainers lined up—'

Henry flexed an arm muscle. 'I could do that. I could be your trainer.'

'Thanks, but I won't be needing you and even if I did, I'd want someone to help me tone up, not a rugby coach like you.'

'You never know. In a competition like that, it might be useful to know how to do a good rugby tackle,' said Henry and Pia nodded in agreement.

'I think these girls have their own tactics,' I said. 'Some of them looked like they'd spent a fortune on fake eyelashes, spray tans, teeth whitening, highlights. They were in to win. The only effort I'd made was that I'd washed my hair. I felt a fake. Nah, not for me.'

My phone bleeped in the background.

'Probably Flo,' said Charlie. 'She said she might come by.'

I glanced at Pia. Flo had come by when Charlie was out collecting the supper with Henry. After a quick hi, she'd gone up to spend the evening with Alexei in his apartment. Now that it looked like Flo had another admirer, I wondered if Charlie had suddenly realised what he might be losing. I glanced at my phone. It was a message from Keira: **Just passing, am outside and realised this is where you live.**

'Oh no,' I said. 'I'm not going to answer.'

We went back to watching the TV and my phone beeped again.

Don't you want to be friends?

Pia glanced over my shoulder at the text. 'Text back, no, I don't. She can't know you're in.'

I felt mean. Here was I, all cosy with my mates, and there was Keira, only just back in the UK, standing outside on her own. I couldn't do it to her. I picked up my phone.

Pia glanced at me. 'You don't have to, you know. You're too nice.'

'Who was it?' asked Charlie.

'Keira.'

'Keira KO not OK?' said Charlie. I'd reminded him of our nickname for her when I told him that she was back in town.

I nodded. 'She's outside. She wants to come in.'

'Want me to go and get her?' he asked.

Pia sighed as I nodded then got up to clear away dishes.

Five minutes later, Charlie was back with Keira. She winked at Henry, grinned at Pia then handed me a bottle of elderflower juice. 'Hi, guys, I couldn't pass so close and not call in,' she said.

'You could,' Pia mouthed at me behind her.

'I'm about to make hot chocolates,' I said. 'Do you want one?'

She shook her head. 'I'm off sugar. I'll have some of the elderflower. It's sugar free. Thanks.'

I got up, went to the breakfast bar and poured her a glass.

Keira followed me over. 'You left pretty swiftly this afternoon. I was hoping to see you after. Compare notes.'

'Aunt Maddie was outside,' I said. 'I didn't want to keep her waiting. How did you get on?'

'Great. Good. Fun. I hope I get through. You?'

'Not great. I decided it's not for me.'

Keira nodded. 'I thought you'd decide that.'

'Why?'

'Well . . . don't forget that I've known you a long time.'

I was quiet for a few moments but it bugged me. What was she insinuating? 'What do you mean? You know me?'

Kiera shrugged a shoulder and turned to watch Henry and Pia who were curled up on the sofa. 'Oh, nothing. I shouldn't have said anything.'

'Oh come on, Keira. You can't say that.' Again, I had a familiar nagging feeling in the pit of my stomach as I remembered how she used to do this when we were younger when she'd make out she knew something or had a secret but wasn't going to tell.

'OK, just, well . . . let's just say I thought you'd drop out. I remember you don't like criticism and you don't like to step outside your comfort zone. To be honest, I don't think you've got what it takes. I don't mean that in a mean way . . . just, you have to be tough to go through with something like this.'

'Are you saying I'm not tough enough?'

'No. OK, yes. You've got to have the right attitude and you're so totally inoffensive. I mean that in a nice way, Jess.'

So why do I feel like you're putting me down? I asked myself.

The landline rang and this time Charlie took the call. He spoke into the phone for a few moments then looked up. 'Alisha wants to know if we want to go up for cheesecake,' he said. 'She wants to see us before they go tomorrow.'

'Yay,' said Henry who had a sweet tooth and could be lured anywhere with pudding.

'Who's Alisha?' asked Keira.

'One of the residents' daughters,' said Henry. 'Jefferson Lewis's daughter.' Pia kicked him. 'Ow. What? What have I done?'

If Keira noticed, she didn't let on. Her face had lit up. 'Are you going to go?'

'I . . . oh . . .'

'Security's really tight up there, Keira,' said Pia. 'Designed by the SAS and you don't want to mess with them.'

Keira rolled her eyes. 'They let you up though, yeah?'

Pia nodded. 'Yes, but we've been friends of Alisha's for a while.'

'Which is exactly why the SAS or whoever won't mind if you OK it with your new friend. Do you think she'd mind if I tagged along, Jess? I won't stay long because as I was just saying, I was only passing.' She got up and went to link arms with Charlie. 'Ask if she minds if you bring a friend, hey?'

Charlie looked at me as if to say, what can I do? I could hear Pia sighing heavily. Henry was oblivious to it all.

'Fine,' I said. 'Ask if we can bring someone.'

Fifteen minutes later, we were up at the Lewises'. The apartment was full of people coming and going: Mr Lewis's PA, Mrs Lewis's masseur, cleaners taking instructions for when the family were away, decorators also being given a job list for while they were away,

Marguerite the housekeeper cooking, a valet packing, the chauffeur confirming times of departure.

Despite all the chaos, Keira had met Mr and Mrs Lewis and had chatted with them briefly about films and the weather and was soon happily sitting up at the breakfast bar between Charlie and JJ and tucking into home-made lime cheesecake, all talk of not eating sugar seemingly forgotten for the moment. I felt so jealous. JJ and Charlie were my two boys – my brother and my almost boyfriend – and she'd managed to muscle in. *I am such a horrible person*, I thought as I watched her flirt with JJ and he laughed at something she said. The scene was my worst nightmare. My first maybe boyfriend and a ghost from my past appears to be whipping him away from under my nose. Even Charlie seemed to be in awe of her. I got up to go to the cloakroom off the hallway.

'Not his type,' said Alisha, appearing behind me just as I opened the cloakroom door.

'Not whose?'

'JJ's,' she said. 'Don't worry. He's done nothing but talk about you these last few days.'

'Really?' I asked. 'Because he's hardly glanced at me this evening.'

'Yes he has! Are you blind? He's been staring at you all night.'

'Keira's stunning though. He's bound to find her attractive.'

'Nah. We've had it drilled into us by Mom and Dad to make new guests welcome. Doesn't mean we like 'em.'

'You don't like her?'

'I don't. She's the type of person who wants to be here because my dad's Jefferson Lewis not because I'm a mate of yours.'

'How can you tell that?'

Alisha tapped her nose. 'Seen it before. She's a user. But hey you, let's not let it bring us down. Let's go and finish the cheesecake.'

She linked my arm and pulled me back into the battleground.

Later than night, I went to check my Facebook messages. There were two. I opened the first which was from JJ.

I was hoping we'd get some time alone but as you saw, it wasn't possible. Such is my life, our family life. There are always a million people around. Always are before we go anywhere. Mom goes into a panic and starts organising everyone. When I'm back I'd still like to take you out and get to know you better. I really like spending time with you. In the meantime, good luck with the competition. Knock 'em dead. Yours JJ X

I wrote back immediately.

Me too. I was hoping for some time alone. Hey ho and away you go. I like spending time with you too and really look forward to seeing you when you're back. Jess XX.

I read it back. *No*, I decided. *Too gushy. I have to stay cool with him and not let him realise just how much I really do like him. That much, I've learnt from Tom. Boys like the chase.*

I deleted my first message and instead wrote back wishing him a good trip and saying I'd see him when he was back. Uber cool and non-committal. I put one X after my name.

I turned to the second message, which was from Keira. *Probably thanking me for the introduction*, I thought as the page opened. Keira had clearly had a great time. Alisha had been true to her word and did what she could to make Keira welcome so I'd told my jealousy to go away and joined in the banter.

I read the first lines of the message.

Dear Jess

It's a drag that I have to write this but you've brought it on yourself with your selfish attitude. Our recent meetings haven't gone well. I think the reason is because we never really got on when we were in junior school and possibly won't ever because you play mind games and always like to be in control of what's happening.

I reread the first lines and felt myself tense.

I'm not happy to be back in London but it's a big place so hopefully I won't ever bump into you again. The competition might have been a problem but you said you're dropping out so that should solve that. You might not have got through anyway because anyone can see that you're not serious about it. You may have thought I was mean to have said that you haven't got what it takes to go on with the competition but I felt I had to tell the truth when you asked .

I thought I'd give you a chance and see how things went after our first meeting outside your school, you blatantly brushed me off. And then when I came to your house you made no effort to really welcome me or offer me any of the take-away you'd just had nor let me get in with your friends. I could tell that you didn't really want me there. I think it's best that we don't see each other again. I didn't trust you back when we were at junior school and I don't trust you or your smiley face and act now. I don't think you have changed at all or grown as a person.

I left my bottle of elderflower at your house and there was about half left so I'd like it back at some point. We don't all have rich friends to give us freshly squeezed juices.

Also, there was some strong chemistry between me and JJ. You probably sensed it so I wanted to add that when he asks me over, I I really don't want to bump into you at the same time.

I felt as if someone had poured cold water over me. I read the message again then burst into tears.

9

The Hunt for Juice

'Do NOT write back,' said Pia when I called her soon after I'd seen Kiera's message. 'She's clearly bonkers. Do NOT engage.'

'But I feel I need to explain—'

'Exactly. That's what she wants. She wants to get a reaction from you but believe me, it will be the wrong reaction in her book. Promise me, you won't write back.'

'I—'

'Promise,' Pia insisted.

'I promise.'

As I snuggled down to try and sleep later that night,

my mind kept going over and over Keira's message. Was any of what she'd accused me of true? Had I been mean to her? Had I blatantly brushed her off? Did I play mind games? It was true that we'd never really got on but neither of us had actually come out and said it. Some things are best left unspoken, Mum always used to say, and if you haven't got something nice to say, then don't say it.

Despite what Pia had said, I felt I had to reply. That was another thing Mum had drummed into me – it was rude not to say anything when someone sent a letter, a message or a gift, or made a phone call. 'Nothing worse than people who just leave you in the air or treat you as if you're invisible,' she'd say. I decided I'd apologise for having upset Keira and say that wasn't my intention. It was true that I hadn't wanted her to come around when she did. I didn't want to share my new life with her. She was right to have picked up on that and although she felt that I wasn't honest in sharing all my feelings, I decided that I would stick with Mum's philosophy and not voice them. I switched on my computer and went to Facebook to read the message again. I saw that there was a new one from her.

L the elderflower juice that I left at your place on the porch outside my house as I don't want to come and collect it. You could ask Charlie to leave it as I don't want to see you. Keira

Blimey, I thought. *And she thought I was controlling. She still owes me six quid too from the day she asked me to buy her sandwich!*

I put my dressing gown on and slipped downstairs. Dad was in the kitchen at the table with a cheese sandwich in front of him. He'd taken off his suit jacket and loosened his tie, a sure sign that at last, he'd clocked off for the day. People say I look more like Dad than Mum. We have the same dark hair and blue eyes and nose. He used to tease me that I had his nose and should give it back because he couldn't smell without it.

'Hello, sweetheart, you're up late.'

I looked at his sandwich. 'You ought to eat properly,' I said. He often got in late and grabbed something quick from the fridge. 'You're supposed to have five a day for good health.' We'd had a lesson in nutrition at school last week – all about eating five portions of fruit and vegetables a day.

He laughed and for a moment looked like a

naughty boy who'd just had a telling-off. 'I know, I know. Can't sleep?'

'I was thirsty,' I said.

'Me too,' said Dad and he pointed at an empty glass in front of him. 'Where did we get the elderflower juice from? It was delicious.'

'No!' I cried. 'Dad, you didn't drink all of it, did you?'

'Yes. Why? What've I done? It was in the fridge.'

'It wasn't ours,' I said.

'Then whose is it and what is it doing in our fridge?'

I felt sick. What if I didn't return the elderflower? Would Keira think it was a mind game or that I'd deliberately drunk it to upset her? I had to find a similar bottle so that I could return it.

Dad looked at me with concern. 'Jess, what's the matter?'

I couldn't tell him. It would sound so stupid. He'd never understand. 'Nothing. Nothing,' I said and turned to go back up the stairs.

'You didn't get a drink. Didn't you want something?' Dad called after me.

'I did but you've just drunk it all.'

'The elderflower? You just said it wasn't ours for drinking. Oh I see. You wanted it.'

'Yes. No. It wasn't ours, Dad. I didn't want it for me. Oh . . . you'll never understand!'

I felt so confused and I could see I'd upset Dad now. He looked bewildered. Part of me wanted him to give me a big hug and tell me it was all right. *I* was all right and not the way Keira saw me. Another part felt cross that he'd drunk the juice, but then why shouldn't he? He was right. It was in our fridge. How could he possibly have known that Keira wanted it back?

I went to my room where Dave, my cat, was lying on the end of the bed. He opened a sleepy eye.

'It's all right for you, matey,' I said. 'Not a care in the world. If I die, I want to come back as a cat!'

'Meow,' said Dave and as I plonked myself on the bed, he got up to nuzzle my hand as if he understood completely and was letting me know that he was on my side.

On Sunday, I got up early and went to the local shop. They didn't sell elderflower juice. I even tried Harrods food hall but although they sold a whole range of juices, they didn't sell the brand that Keira had brought round.

I went home and looked it up on the internet in

the hope that I could find where it was sold locally but no luck. *This is mad*, I thought after an hour, *so despite Pia's advice, I'm just going to come clean with Keira.*

Dear Keira, I'm sorry that we didn't get on and I am sorry if I upset you, it was never my intention. I will respect your wish and not contact you again. I am very sorry that I can't return your juice as my dad came home, saw it in the fridge, thought it was ours and drank it. I did try and find another bottle the same but couldn't, then I remembered that you borrowed six pounds from me the day you forgot your purse so if you keep that, then we should be square. Hope that's all right with you. Good luck with the rest of the competition, Love Jess.

I deleted the love. We weren't close. I didn't love her.

I wrote, with best wishes. I deleted that too. It sounded too formal.

In the end, I put an X after Jess and pressed reply.

A message came back almost instantly.

I didn't realise you were keeping a list of what I owed you. Forget about the juice. I think you're very sad and stingy and hope you feel better soon.

She didn't even sign her name, never mind love, best wishes or an X. She written that I should forget about the juice as if it was me who'd made a thing of it.

I felt I couldn't do anything right.

10

Round Two

At school on Monday, the teen model competition was once more the talk of the corridors. Everyone wanted to know all about it. What Tanisha had said, what she wore, what was next. Janie Tonkin even wanted to do a piece on Flo and me for the school magazine because we were the only two still in. I didn't have the heart to tell them that whatever happened, I wasn't going any further, partly because I didn't want to stand in front of the judges again and partly because I didn't want to see Keira if both of us got through to the next round. At assembly, I glanced around. It was weird. There were some seriously amazing-looking girls at our school. Not conventionally pretty like girls in magazines but with their own beauty and sense of style, like Tamara Quinlan in Lower Sixth. She was big and sassy and a laugh a minute. Everyone loved her, boys especially, but she wouldn't even have got through round one of Catwalk Teen Queen because she was size sixteen. Carrie Barker. A tiny girl with a face so pretty, I liked just looking at her. She'd never have got through either because she was four foot ten. So many girls, interesting-looking girls, all shapes, all sizes. None of them would have made it because they didn't fit the criteria.

As I was coming out of assembly, Mrs Callaghan, our headmistress, called me over.

'Jess,' she said. 'I hear you've entered a modelling competition?'

I nodded and wondered if she was going to tell me to drop it because of the coming exams.

'Excellent, in that case, you're just the man for the job. And Florence of course. I've got a project for you. At the end of term, we want to stage our own modelling show. Not a competition, just a show to raise funds. With your experience, you'd be the perfect people to organise it. What do you think?'

'I . . .' I knew Mrs Callaghan well enough to know that an enquiry like that didn't mean, could you help? It meant, you *will* help. 'Of course.'

'Pick a theme. Pick your team. We'll talk later.' And off she went, leaving me in a panic. Theme? Team? Where would I start? We'd have to pick models. *Oh crap,* I thought. *Everyone will want to be in it and we'll alienate anyone who is picked. We'll be the most unpopular girls in school!*

In the evening as I was getting home from school, I saw Tanisha get out of a car at the front. She saw me and waved for me to stop. A couple of men that were passing did a double take when they saw her. As always she looked stunning, in a black leather mac, knee-high suede boots which made her legs look endless and her dark hair cascading down her back.

'Hey, Jess, how's it going?' she said as she came close.

'Er. Good.'

'Did you enjoy the session on Saturday?'

'I . . . oh yes,' I lied. Keira was so right. I wasn't an honest person. But the teen competition was Tanisha's thing, I couldn't tell her that I was finding it really uncomfortable. For the hundredth time that week, I wished Mum was around to talk it over with. She'd have been able to tell me how to deal with it all.

'You'll be hearing the day after tomorrow,' she said then she winked. 'I think you're in with a good chance, Jess. A very good chance. You made the judges laugh and we're looking for personality as well as looks.'

'Hun-neugh,' I said. I was surprised. I thought I'd blown it with the judges completely.

Tanisha looked at me. 'Hun-neugh?'

I nodded. 'It's gobbledy-gook for that's great.'

Tanisha cracked up. 'Hah! Say, do you want to come up and see what I've done with my apartment?'

Now that I didn't have to lie about. 'Me? You bet!'

'Got five minutes now?'

I nodded. She indicated that I should follow her into reception, and into the lift.

'I've got to host a modelling show,' I blurted as we stepped inside. 'For school, end-of-term, fundraiser kind of thing.'

'So you're after my job?' Tanisha asked with a smile.

'Oh no! My headmistress asked me because she thinks I've got the experience now that I've entered your competition. As if.'

'It *will* be good experience, Jess. You'll learn a lot and if you do the show at school right, you'll have a

111

lot of fun. Hard work but fun. Just ask me if you need any advice.'

'I will. I have to pick a theme of sorts and I haven't even begun to think about it yet.'

'Get a good team behind you for starters,' said Tanisha as we stepped out of the lift on to her floor and made our way down the plush carpeted corridor to her apartment.

'I've seen a few of the apartments,' I said as she let me in. 'They're all so different.'

'I have a few homes around the world,' said Tanisha. 'They're all so different too.'

'Really? Where?'

'A beach apartment in LA. It's all wood and seaside colours, you know? Blue and sand. I have a penthouse in the village in New York that's traditional, big sofas, old paintings, and I have a little chill-out place in St Lucia and now this is home too. My designer did all my places but I told him to go for gold with this one.'

She beckoned me inside. 'Have a look around and I'll fix us a juice. Do you like fresh orange?'

'Love it,' I said. I couldn't believe my luck. I was in Tanisha's apartment, she was chatting away to me like we were best buddies and she'd given me permission to have a nose around. I couldn't wait to tell Meg, Flo and

Pia. Her apartment was lovely. Parquet floors, sumptu-ous gold velvet sofas in her living room, with the same floor-to-ceiling windows that all the apartments at the back had and a sliding door that opened out onto a terrace with views over the park. The gilt furniture and mirrors that Pia and I had seen when she first moved in had been strategically placed and gave the place an opulent look. I loved the way that every room ran into the next through tall folding wooden doors. There was a king-size ivory sleigh bed with a gold silk spread in a spacious bedroom with a dressing room off one side and an enormous en-suite sand-coloured marble bathroom on the other. In every room were life-size glossy photos of various front covers that Tanisha had done: *Vogue*, *Harper's*, *Tatler*. At the front was a mirrored room with gym equipment with Tanisha's Grammy awards on one wall and a ton of others lining the wall opposite. It was the perfect pop diva's flat and like all the apartments, it smelt wonderful, like an ocean breeze.

'Like it?' asked Tanisha when I went to join her in the kitchen, which was cosier than some of the others I'd seen as the décor she'd chosen was oak and a honey-coloured granite.

'Love it. What's it like for you travelling all the time?'

Tanisha sighed and smiled. 'It's part of the job. I'm one of the lucky ones though. I can afford to get a place like this and make it home. It wasn't such fun in the beginning. Believe me, the allure of staying in hotels, no matter how fancy, wears thin after a while and yeah, I get lonely sometimes, that's the price I pay, but hey, it's the life I chose and I ain't complaining.' She handed me my juice. 'And I miss my mom.'

She looked sad. 'Me too,' I said.

'You do? I thought you lived in the block. Where is she?'

'She died just over a year ago . . .' I felt myself fill up with tears. 'I . . . I'm so sorry. I don't usually cry about it. I—'

Tanisha came round the breakfast bar and gave me a hug. 'Hey, you cry all you want, hon. I lost my dad a few years back and just when you think you're OK, it jumps out at you like a big ole tiger who's been waiting in the bush.'

I sniffed back my tears. 'I wish she was round to talk to.'

'So who was that lady you left with after the competition?'

'Oh, she's my aunt Maddie. Mum's sister.'

'So it's just you and your daddy?'

I nodded. 'And my brother Charlie.' I suddenly had the most brilliant idea! Dad and Tanisha. It was about time he had a girlfriend. All he ever did was work, work, work and he wasn't bad-looking when he made an effort. 'Do you want to come by and meet him properly one night?'

'Sure,' she said then laughed. 'Say, you're not going to try and fix me up, are you?'

I laughed, a bit too hysterically. 'Me? No! As if!'

Luckily my phone beeped that I had a text before Tanisha noticed that I was blushing as well. It was Dad asking where I was.

'I'd better go, Tanisha. Dad just texted that my gran's arrived so I should make a move. Thanks for the juice.'

'Anytime, hon,' she said. 'Nice talking to you. You have a nice time with your family now.'

As I made my way downstairs, I thought about how normal she seemed, behind the diva persona, and I could see that she would get lonely sometimes being on her own – her apartment so quiet and neat in comparison to the lived-in feel at the Lewises'. I wished I could have talked to her honestly about the competition and Keira but I felt that would be unfair, like being a snitch, and I didn't want Tanisha thinking that I was telling tales on other contestants to gain an advantage.

But oh God, what now? I asked my reflection in the lift's mirrored interior. Tanisha had indicated that I'd got through to the next round and after our conversation, my excuses for backing out seemed hollow. Mum, what would you tell me to do? I don't want to be the type of person who doesn't see things through but I don't want to see Kiera either.

I wished I had someone to talk to about it. Of course there were my mates but I wanted to talk to a grown-up. Dad wasn't an option. He'd be worried about Keira dissing me, make a big deal out of it and might do or say something embarrassing if he saw her. And there was Aunt Maddie, but even though I was getting on loads better with her lately, I had a feeling that she'd say back out but for different reasons to mine. She wasn't into fashion and felt that so much of that whole world was exploitation. Mum had worked in the fashion business and would have understood the pluses and minuses.

When I got back to the house, there was a wonderful aroma of onions and garlic cooking and Gran was busy at the breakfast bar chopping peppers.

'I'm making supper,' she said. 'Chicken casserole. Make sure you're eating right.'

'Sheila makes sure we do that,' I said then I pulled a face. Sheila was the housekeeper who came in a few times a week to make meals for Charlie and me seeing as Dad never had a moment to do anything like cook. Her meals were OK but a bit bland and she only seemed to know how to do pasta, shepherd's pie and baked potatoes. I sniffed the air. It smelt delicious, Gran was a great cook. 'But it will be nice to have a change from macaroni cheese.'

'Now come on, sit down, tell me what's been going on.'

'Where are Dad and Charlie?' I asked.

'Charlie's not back yet and your dad's just popped back to his office. Some minor crisis with a resident's plumbing.'

'Great,' I said. 'So I've got you all to myself.' *Of course*, I thought, *Gran. She's the perfect person to talk to.* Like Mum used to, she always sees both sides of things. Because she's a Libran, she says. 'So do you want to go first or do I?'

'You,' she said. 'You talk, I'll chop.'

'OK but I want to know all your news as well,' I said. Listening as well as talking was another thing that Mum had drummed into Charlie and me. 'It's impolite and boring to talk about yourself non-stop like you're the only person on the planet that anything's ever happened to,' she'd tell us. 'Everyone has their story, their worries and hopes.' Sometimes when Charlie or I would come home with a major drama, she'd put the timer on and give us five minutes. Then when the *ping* went that time was up, she'd set it again and she'd talk for five minutes about her day. It used to calm us down. I also knew Mum had learnt to do this from Gran.

Right on cue, Gran put the timer on. We smiled at each other, completely in tune with each other's thought.

'Go,' she said.

I settled myself on a stool at the bar and filled her in on the whole story. Keira. Our past. The competition. My fears. Tanisha.

She listened without interrupting, just nodding here and there until the timer pinged that my time was up.

'So what do you think?' I asked.

Gran put down the knife she'd been chopping with, put green leaves into a salad bowl then turned to face me.

'Go for it, Jess.' She sounded so like Mum sometimes, her voice had exactly the same tone. It was comforting and distressing at the same time. 'First of all, I don't like to think of anyone being mean to you. I know you well and you have a sweet and generous nature. I hate to think that someone's making you doubt yourself and your motives. I'd like to get a bottle of that precious elderflower and pour it over that silly girl's head. You mustn't give up just because you don't want to run into someone who's a bully.'

'I wouldn't call her a bully, Gran.'

Gran shook her head. 'There are bullies that use their fists and there are bullies that use their minds. The damage the second kind do isn't physical but they do damage all the same. They wear away someone's confidence with jibes and teasing then deny it all and make it sound as if it's the fault of the person they're teasing. I'd say, give that girl a run for her money in the competition and DON'T let her intimidate you!'

'But I hate confrontation, Gran.'

'What's your option? You're going to let her wear you down? No. There's a time you have to take a stand and make it clear that you're not a coward nor are you the type of person who gives up when the going gets tough. This is that time. The Jess I know doesn't run away and whimper. By giving up, you're letting her win. That's not the girl I know.' Gran grinned and pressed the timer. 'OK, my turn, but just before I take it, what's your decision?'

I put out my left palm to high-five Gran. 'I won't give up.'

11

Learning How to Walk

'OK. Number eleven. Go,' called Jacob Johnson, the image coach who had been brought in to show the twenty finalists how to walk the catwalk. I was one of them. Keira looked surprised when I came through the doors with Flo in the morning, raised an eyebrow and said something to a blonde girl she seemed to have palled up with. I smiled at her like I was so cool and not fazed by the messages she'd sent. All of us knew who Jacob was, having seen him on various TV makeover shows. He was a small, skinny blond and always dressed in black with heeled boots. I liked him because he treated each one of us like we were his favourite girlfriend. I was number fifteen. Keira was sixteen. Flo had already done her trial walk and she'd sauntered down the catwalk like she was walking through a field of flowers. Jacob had told her to put more attitude into it.

'No, no, NO,' called Jacob as number eleven, a tall redhead, walked towards him. I felt sorry for her because she looked so nervous, her face tight with concentration, her body awkward. It didn't help that we all had to walk in four-inch heels. I was already wobbling in mine. 'OK, everyone. Listen up. Look and learn. Our girl here is too tight. You need to loosen up, keep your eyes ahead, long steps, no horse-stepping, no short steps. I want you all to relax and enjoy this. It's your moment. So who's next? Number twelve. Go girl.'

'It doesn't look easy,' whispered Flo as the next girl went forward to take her turn.

'No, NO. Stop,' called Jacob as she sashayed towards him. 'Too sexy. Tone it down. You're a goddess, you're unreachable. The way you're rolling your hips, you're telling the world that you're anybody's. Oh Lord!' The girl went over on one ankle and tumbled to the floor and Jacob rushed to help her up. She was already in tears.

I glanced over in Keira's direction. 'Eek,' I mouthed and nodded my head at the fallen girl. She looked the other way.

Girl number twelve was helped to a seat and number thirteen was up ready.

'Close your mouth, close your mouth,' called Jacob as she stiffly made her way towards him. 'You're not catching flies! Now relax, you're walking like one of the undead.'

Number fourteen was up next. 'You're waddling. I said to loosen up but not *that* much,' Jacob commented then demonstrated how we should walk. 'See, it has to come from the eyes then the body will follow. Eyes ahead.' The girl tried again. 'No. No,' Jacob sighed. 'Now you're walking like a monkey.' The poor girl looked like she didn't know what to do with her arms or legs and I almost had a fit of the giggles.

'Number fifteen,' called Jacob.

'Here I go,' I said as Flo helped steady me on the heels. 'He'll probably say I walk like a duck.'

'Quack,' said Flo.

I went and took my place at the top of the room.

'OK, go,' Jacob instructed. 'Drop your shoulders, that's it.'

When I was little, Mum and I used to play that we were models. It used to crack us up. Before she got ill, Mum worked as a personal stylist at Selfridges and used to attend all the big fashion shows. I went to a few with her when I was old enough and we often used to pretend we were on the catwalk on the way home. *Here I go, Mum,* I thought, *this time it's for real.* I stood tall, fixed my eyes at the end of the room, took a deep breath and walked.

'OK, good. Sink into your hips a little,' called Jacob. 'That's it. As you come to the end of the runway, stop with a stomp. Lean on one hip and pow! Not bad, not bad. NEXT.'

I'd done it. I glanced over at Flo. She gave me the thumbs up.

The rest of the morning was fun. Racks of clothes had been brought in and we had to practise doing quick changes then out on the catwalk again. Flo and I both found it easy-peasy scrambling into clothes, having got dressed in a hurry a million times when we were late for school. A few girls looked ill at ease getting changed in front of each other but I didn't mind that either. We did it every week in the cloakroom when getting ready for sports practice.

Towards the end of the morning, it was line-up time again and we all had to go and stand in front of the judges and Tanisha who'd crept in at the back towards the end of the rehearsal. We listened as the judges gave their comments.

'Wow, this is personal,' I whispered to Flo as one girl was told that she needed to get her hair straightened. Another was told she had bad skin. Another that her hair was too thin and straggly.

'Your eyes are dead,' said Derek to a stunning blonde girl who looked taken aback by his comment.

'Your worry comes through in your eyes,' said Jackie to a black girl with short hair.

'You're too heavy on the bottom,' said Karie to a blonde girl with a beautiful heart-shaped face. 'If you're going to stay in, you have to lose some padding.'

The girl looked perfect to me.

'Too heavy on the top,' Derek told a curvy black girl.

'You walk like a horse,' Jackie told a waif-like girl with huge eyes and wispy white hair.

I felt my jaw dropping. Here were the most beautiful girls being told that they weren't good enough. Part of me wanted to say, oi, if you haven't got something nice to say, don't say it, but another part felt they were just doing their job. I thought about the girls I'd been looking at in school assembly earlier in the week. The judges would have had a field day with them – too fat, too thin, too small, too . . . just not right. It sucked that anyone should be made to feel that way. I'd read somewhere that sixty-five per cent of the population were size sixteen plus. *There should be a modelling contest for them*, I thought. *And not just them. For all sorts. All shapes and sizes, big and small.*

The judges turned to Flo. 'Ah Florence,' said Karie. 'Slightly nervous? Don't be. You're a very pretty girl but we feel that your look is bland. You need an edge. An attitude. Think you can work on that?'

Flo nodded and then they turned to me.

'Jessica. You need to be more confident. We feel that you don't really think that you deserve to be here,' said Jackie. 'Own your place here. A lack of confidence doesn't wash in the modelling world. You have to act and sell the product no matter how you're feeling inside. OK?'

I nodded. *Own my place? How the heck am I supposed to do that?* I wondered.

The waif-like girl was in floods of tears after the judges and Tanisha left to confer and we waited to hear who'd been eliminated. 'It's my whole life, my dream, my everything,' she told us.

'Someone's throwing up in the loo,' said the redhead when she came back from the cloakroom. 'Eating disorder or nerves, do you think?'

'Probably both,' said her friend. 'That's so last decade. I think the trend is to look healthier these days and anyway, throwing up messes up your teeth.'

'How come?' asked the redhead.

'The acid from vomit erodes your teeth over time and throwing up can make the glands in your neck swell and give you ulcers. I should know. I tried it until I realised it was actually making me look and feel crap.'

Ew, I thought. I felt more and more like a fraud as I overheard how important it was to the other contestants. I couldn't say it had ever been my dream to be a model. In fact, I still had no idea what I wanted to do when I left school.

Finally we were called into a back room and told to line up in front of the judges. They stared at us. We stared at them.

Tanisha stood up. 'Well done, everyone. You've all worked very hard today but this is a competition and I'm afraid five of you won't be coming back.' She stayed silent for a while as we waited to hear which of us hadn't got through. It was just like being on *The X Factor* or *Strictly Come Dancing* when the contestants were kept in agony as they prolonged the results. I felt like I was going to get the giggles again. I always did in tense situations. *Don't laugh, don't laugh,* I told myself.

'I'm going to put you in groups of five,' Tanisha said then read out four groups of names. I was in the third group.

More silence. More trying to suppress the need to laugh. I daren't look at Flo who was in group two along with Keira. I knew if I caught Flo's eye, I'd burst out laughing. Not that I thought the situation was funny at all. It wasn't. It was excruciating.

Once we were in our four groups, Tanisha surveyed us all with no expression on her face. 'Group two, you're through,' she said finally.

The girls exploded with relief. More silence as Tanisha looked at the remaining groups. 'Group four, you're through.'

There were more sighs of relief and hugging. 'Group one . . .' More silence. The atmosphere was so tense, it was as if time had stood still and all you could hear was people's breathing. 'Group one . . . you'll be going home today.'

'*Oh!*' they chorused with disappointment while girls in my group realised that they'd made it and were through.

Flo came over and hugged me. 'I can't believe it,' she said.

'Me neither,' said a voice behind us.

I turned to see Keira standing there.

'Oh hi, Keira.'

'I suppose it helps living in the same place as the main sponsor,' she said.

'I . . .'

'Hey, that's not fair,' said Flo. 'I'm sure Tanisha had nothing to do with Jess getting through. There are three other judges and they don't live at Porchester Park.'

'Yeah sure,' said Keira with a sneer. 'Anyway, I thought you were dropping out.'

'I was going to,' I replied. I was about to tell her about my conversation with Tanisha then realised then it really would look like I had friends in high places.

'So what made you change your mind?' asked Keira.

'I'm not someone who gives up easily—' I started.

Keira snorted. 'Hah! Why should you when you live in a place with A-listers on your door and running into Tanisha every day.'

'It's not like that, Keira,' I said. 'Actually it hasn't

always been easy living there but . . .' I didn't want to open up to her and tell her about how it had been when I'd first moved there. She'd only find some way to misinterpret what I was saying.

'Poor little rich girl, that's you,' said Kiera.

'Why are you being so horrible?' asked Flo. 'What did Jess ever do to you? I think you're just jealous.'

Keira looked down her nose at me. 'Me? As if. What's there to be jealous of? I was only there five minutes and clearly JJ liked me and your other—'

'Says who?' interrupted Flo.

'Says me,' said Keira. 'And don't think that JJ is yours just because you live in the same place, Jess. You don't own him or any part of him.'

I was about to say that I had a date with JJ when he came back from LA but bit my tongue. I didn't want to tell her anything. 'Come on, Flo, let's go,' I said and pulled her away. I felt confused. No-one had ever talked to me the way that Keira had, like she really hated me. I didn't understand why.

I turned back to her. 'Listen, we're both in this competition. Why can't we at least try to get along? We're all in it together.'

'Not me,' said Keira. 'I'm in this to win and I'm not in it together with anyone.'

She turned and walked off. Flo stuck her tongue out after her.

'Take no notice, Jess,' she said. 'She's just mean.'

I nodded but it was too late. She got under my skin. The way she treated me hurt. I also got the feeling she'd been about to say something else before Flo had interrupted but I told myself not to dwell on it and to try and get her and her behaviour out of my mind.

12

Finding a Look

'I have to own my place,' I told the gathered family at lunch at Gran's on Sunday. 'And Flo was told she's too bland and has to find her look. I'll probably have to do that too so that I stand out from the rest of the competitors.'

'Shave your eyebrows off,' said Charlie. 'That'll make you look different.'

'I can always rely on you for style advice. Not.'

'So what happens next?' asked Aunt Maddie who was looking most unimpressed by everything I'd said about the competition. 'And what about your swimming? I thought that was your thing. Don't you have to practise for upcoming events?'

I shook my head. 'There's nothing now until the end of the year. The team just has to stay fit and practise regularly, that's all.'

'So what's next with the modelling?' asked Gran.

'There are fifteen of us who've got through so far. In the next round, we have our photos taken and then five more go out, then the finalists will have their shots go onto the competition website and the public can vote. On the last week, we get to do a catwalk show and all the audience there can add their vote too. Whoever has the most votes gets a spread in *Teen in the City* magazine and five thousand pounds.'

'Yay,' said Charlie. 'Hope you win. What would you do with the dosh?'

'I haven't thought about it because I'm not going to win. No way. There are some seriously gorgeous girls in the running.'

'Cool. Ask them all over for supper,' said Charlie. 'But don't diss yourself. I reckon you're in with a chance.'

I shook my head. 'Some of the girls already have personal trainers and go for regular beauty treatments and their make-up is the best you can buy.'

'Yeah but we'll get everyone at school to vote,' said Charlie.

'Maybe, but don't forget there's Flo too. Some people at school will vote for her.'

'How's she doing?' asked Charlie.

'Good. She's enjoying it.'

'Is she still seeing the Russian prince?' he asked.

'Is he a prince?' asked Gran.

'No,' said Dad who up until then had been more intent on his roast dinner than the conversation. He didn't often get to sit down and eat properly so he was enjoying it.

'Why do you ask about Flo?' I asked Charlie. 'Do you care?'

'No,' he said but he blushed. Hah. He did care. I wondered if I should tell her. She'd had a crush on him for so long but given up because he never seemed to be bothered, plus her confidence had taken a knock from his lack of interest. Being with Alexei was good for her along with the modelling competition. She was beginning to realise what a gorgeous girl she was. If I told her about Charlie being interested after all, it might mess things up with Alexei, and even though I'd been taken with him in the beginning, I had to admit, they made a lovely couple.

'And are you confident?' asked Gran.

'That's what they asked,' I said. 'The judges' comments were that I had to own my place in the competition.'

'Nothing wrong with owning your place,' said Aunt Maddie, 'but I don't like the idea of you being judged. Any of you. Contests like this set up a precedent and if you don't fit the bill, you're made to feel as if you're not worthy.'

It was typical of Aunt Maddie to say something like that. In fact, I was surprised that she hadn't been demonstrating with banners out in front of the building where the contest was being held. She liked a cause. She's green, she's vegetarian, she's into equality, feminism, she's pro this and against that. For once though, I agreed with her.

'Exactly what I thought, Aunt M. You should have seen the state of some of the girls who didn't get through. It was as if someone had told them they were ugly as Shrek. I don't like that aspect either. Like at our school, eighty per cent of our class wouldn't have qualified because they aren't tall enough or are the wrong shape but each one of them has their own style and look. I hate that they are made to feel excluded.'

Aunt Maddie looked aghast. 'You're agreeing with me?'

I nodded.

She laughed and shook her head. 'Well, that's a first.'

'Seems to me,' said Gran, 'that everyone's got something lovely about them but very few people get the whole package.'

I nodded. 'I was thinking that at school last week. Like Kay Bryston in our class has got a killer body but a sharp nose and jaw. Janie Pierson's got the most beautiful eyes but a thin mouth and nightmare frizzy hair. Sarah Callagher's got a wide full mouth to die for but her eyes are bit close together. Her mate Amy's got long glossy hair but bad skin and other girls have got great flat stomachs but big bums or thighs and others have got great bums and legs but have tummies.'

Gran laughed. 'Nobody is ever happy with what they're given. The trick is to make the most of what you've got. If you dress right, you can distract from any flaws, and make-up can accentuate the positive. Flaunt what you've got. Cover the rest and hairdressers can do anything with hair these days.'

Aunt Maddie frowned. 'It's not right. You say distract from flaws. Who says they're flaws? Who says a big bum isn't beautiful?'

Dad and Charlie had exchanged glances and were clearly having a hard time not laughing out loud.

'It's all the fault of the media,' Aunt Maddie continued. I could see she was revving up for one of her rants. 'They only put skinny waifs in their magazines. They're not representative of normal girls. In Rubens' time, back in the seventeenth century, big and curvy was thought to be beautiful and was the fashion then. Now it's thin and size zero. Fashions are always changing and it's wrong because it alienates anyone who doesn't fit the latest whim of some dictatorial magazine editor.'

'Ah, it's all a bit of fun,' said Gran. 'I was in a modelling competition once you know.'

'You, Mum? You never said,' said Aunt Maddie.

Gran tapped her nose. 'You don't know everything about me. I was very young, before I was married.'

'Did you win?' I asked.

'I did,' said Gran. 'I didn't pursue it though. I had a place at art school and was more interested in that.'

'I'm not surprised you won,' I said. Even in her mid-sixties, Gran was striking-looking. She was tall and elegant with silver white hair cut in a bob and she always wore lovely Bohemian clothes and big ethnic jewellery. Mum had inherited her looks and sense of style but up until recently, Aunt Maddie had always rejected fashion as being trivial. A few weeks ago though, Pia and I'd managed a makeover on her and we'd persuaded her to have her mousy brown hair cut into layers and highlighted. She'd also been making an effort to get out of her normal jeans and fleeces and today, although she was wearing jeans, they weren't as baggy as usual and she had a sweet pale green cardigan on.

'Thank you, Jess,' said Gran. 'If you can keep things in perspective throughout the competition, then it's fine. If you don't get through, don't feel that you've failed and that you're not beautiful. I know if your mum was here, she'd be championing you all the way but telling you to stay grounded at the same time. You mustn't let any of it go to your head.'

'Not much chance of that,' I said. 'It is fun in one way but all the contestants have to take a lot of criticism as well.'

'That's what I mean,' said Gran. 'Keep things in perspective. You're much more than a pretty face, Jess. I think that what truly makes a person beautiful is how they treat other people.' She gave me a pointed look. I knew she was talking about Keira but was sensitive enough to know that I wouldn't want to talk about it in front of everyone. As I helped clear the plates, I thought about Keira and the way that she was treating me, or was it me who was treating her badly? Even though I was trying to not let her intimidate me, I still felt that she twisted things around so that it seemed as if I was the mean one and I'd begun to wonder if there was any truth in that. I'd had another sleepless night last night, going over and over what she'd said, what I'd said, how I'd been with her, and asking myself if, unintentionally, I had been mean to her. The whole business was making me feel very anxious and unsure of myself. Pia says that some people just get you, your sense of humour and the intention behind what you say. Some people don't and misinterpret everything. Simple as that. Sometimes I wished that I had her uncomplicated view on life. All the same, I was so grateful that I had my bunch of mates, and especially Pia, who *did* get me and never took what I said the wrong way.

'Exactly, true beauty comes from within,' said Aunt Maddie. 'We need to see more real women in magazines and in the media too.'

'True, but this is a modelling contest, so my advice, Jess,' Gran continued, 'is simply be yourself. Don't try to be anyone else or copy anyone else's style. The best become the best by being themselves.'

'Clothes look better on tall and thin,' said Dad. 'Fact.'

'Says who?' exploded Aunt Maddie. 'You men, you're all the same. You can't see beyond a female's looks.'

Dad ducked down a bit and put his hand up as if to protect himself but he was laughing. He liked to wind Aunt Maddie up. 'No harm in appreciating what's beautiful.'

Aunt Maddie threw a piece of bread at him. *My family are all children*, I thought as I pulled off a piece of bread and joined in.

After lunch, I went up to Gran's room and took a long look at myself in the mirror. I felt that I was nothing special, in fact I'd always felt that it was Charlie who had the best looks in our family, having inherited Mum's fine bone structure and lovely copper-coloured eyes.

'You look bland,' I said to my reflection. 'You need to do something.' In the mirror, I saw a tall, slim girl with long chestnut hair which today had a kink in it due to the damp weather. My hair drove me mad because it always went wonky when it rained. I also looked pale and washed out after the long, cold winter. I thought about what Gran had said about being myself. Mum used to say the same thing. *Being myself doesn't mean letting it all go though*, I thought. *I have different selves. The washed-out winter me when my hair needs a wash, my skin's breaking out in spots, my legs need waxing and I'm wearing trackie bottoms and an old T-shirt, and then there's the dressed-up me when I've made an effort, am wearing something nice, have shiny hair and clear skin.*

A plan was forming in my head. I would be myself for the competition but I'd be my best self. My Sunday best self – starting with my skin. If anyone in the competition needed a spray tan, it was me. I stared hard at myself in the mirror and wondered what else I could do to improve my looks without changing myself. I had cornflower blue eyes which Mum said were my best feature. I could dye my eyelashes so that if we had to do any session in the competition without make-up, I'd still look decent. I had a wide mouth which looked even bigger with lipgloss. I could get one of the make-up brands that plumps up lips even more. Models always seemed to have the bee-stung look. I didn't like my nose and had always felt it was too big – not much I can do about that! My body's

OK. Not a killer hourglass body like Kay at school's with her tiny waist but I was slim with a medium bust. My shoulders were on the broad side from swimming but Pia said that's good for modelling.

I found a piece of paper and made a list. I had my plan. A DIY makeover to make the most of what I've got. I might not be able to afford beauty treatments at an expensive salon, or a personal trainer, but Mum had always taught me that you didn't need money to have a beauty sesh. What you did need was a bit of imagination and ability to be creative with what was in the cupboard. We often used to sit and watch telly at the weekend with a honey and yoghurt face mask on and she'd never let an avocado be thrown in the bin. She'd rather put it on her face, mashed up and used as a moisturiser. I'd take a leaf out of her book. I could spend my pocket money on a few shop-bought products but I'd see if I could find some of Mum's home-made beauty product recipes too.

13

DIY Beauty Session

'Oweeeeee!' I cried as Pia ripped the waxing paper off my right leg.

'Oh don't be such a wimp,' she said as she ripped at another strip. 'You have to suffer to be beautiful.'

She'd been very enthusiastic about my plan when I'd told her, and we'd been to Boots after school on Monday and bought all the items on my list: a home waxing kit, a spray-on tan, serum for plumper lips, eyelash tint and a deep-moisturising face mask. We were going to have a beautification evening in the VIP shed at my house. We'd decked it out like a proper salon with all our products lined up; we'd even put on a relaxation CD like they do in some salons in order to create a calm atmosphere.

'Do you want me to do your arms as well?' she asked as Dave watched with a bewildered expression on his face. I stroked his head. 'Don't worry, Dave. We're not going to wax you!'

'Meow,' he said. I think he was agreeing that bald wasn't a good look on a cat.

I glanced down at my arms. They weren't hairy but I wanted to be silky smooth. 'OK, go on then. I want to be the gloss Queen with shiny hair and clear, soft, sun-kissed skin.'

'And so it shall be,' said Pia as she applied wax to my arms then once again ripped away. It didn't hurt as much as my legs and Pia was quick and good at it. Her mum had worked in the beauty industry most of her life so Pia had grown up watching her do facials, waxings and eyelash tints. I trusted her completely.

After I was waxed smooth as a baby's bum, it was time for the spray tan and we were going to take turns with each other as Pia had been looking pale too. We stripped down to our underwear and placed towels under our feet.

'Stand about a foot away,' I told Pia when she aimed the can of spray tan at me.

'Shame Flo and Meg couldn't make it,' I said. We'd invited them to come back with us but Meg had karate practice and Flo had a music lesson.

'I know. We could have looked like we'd all been on the same holiday,' said Pia. 'How much of this stuff do you put on?'

'Not sure. Until you're a good colour I guess,' I said when it was her turn and I aimed the can at her. Once we'd sprayed all over, we stood back to survey our work.

'Nothing seems to be happening,' said Pia. 'Maybe it's a dud can.'

'Give me another coat,' I said, 'and I'll do you again too though it's hard to tell properly in this light.'

We sprayed each other again but we both still looked winter white. 'Never mind,' said Pia. 'We can go and get another stronger brand tomorrow. Maybe some work better than others or you have to have a bit of a tan to start with.'

I gave my face a third coat for good luck then we turned to the business of eyelash tinting. I painted Pia's and then she painted mine.

'Ow. It stings,' I said as some of the mixture dribbled into my eyes.

'Keep your eyes shut then, dummy,' said Pia. 'It only stings while it's going on then we have to lie still for five minutes.'

'I think I might do my eyebrows too,' I said and painted the leftover dye on my eyebrows. 'I've seen in magazines that models have really well defined brows.'

After we'd applied the tint, we lay on the rug.

'I'm glad you've taken this positive approach,' said Pia.

'I am. I feel a lot better about it now, like, all you can do is give it your best shot. To begin with, I was unsure how I felt about this competition, like on Sunday, I was beginning to wonder what I was trying to prove and was it worth it.'

'And is it?'

I nodded. 'I think so. I wanted to do something to lift me out of the ordinary, you know? Like to be in with a chance with JJ or Tom, although I am so not interested in him now, but boys like that, they want someone special.'

Pia was quiet for a while. 'Are you saying that I'm ordinary because I'm not in the competition?'

'What? No! I felt I was ordinary before it all started.'

'But by being in for a modelling competition, you're not ordinary any more, now you're special. That sounds like you're leaving me behind.'

'No. That is so *not* what I meant at all.' I tried to open my eyes to see Pia's face but the minute I did, the tint ran in and made my eyes sting again. 'Ow. Ow.'

Once the five minutes was up, we cleaned our eyes and it did seemed to have worked although my eyes were a bit red.

'Don't worry about that,' said Pia. 'It'll wear off.' She glanced at her watch. 'I have to go, so, see you in the morning at the bus stop, yeah?'

I nodded. 'I haven't upset you, have I? I don't think I'm special by doing this.'

Pia shrugged. 'You know the saying – two mistakes you can make in life. One is to think that you're special, the other is to think that you're not.'

I laughed but after Pia had left and I'd gone inside the house, I wondered if I had been insensitive and resolved to be more careful about what I said in future. I didn't want anyone thinking I was getting too big for my boots.

Before getting into bed, I applied the deep mois- turising mask then went down to the kitchen to get some olive oil. I'd read that if you apply it to your hair and leave it in a towel overnight, you get wonderfully glossy locks. I searched the kitchen but couldn't see olive oil, only sunflower. *That'll do*, I decided and took it up to my room where I applied it liberally then wrapped my head in a towel ready for bed. I did look funny with my white mask on and head in a turban. I decided to leave the mask on overnight as well as the oil because I'd heard that the longer you leave them on, the more effective they are. I placed another towel over my pillow then settled down for the night. Dave had followed me up and had settled on the end of my bed. He looked quite bewildered by my appearance.

'It's going to be worth it,' I told him. 'I'm going to wake up looking my Sunday best self.'

'Meow,' he replied and gave me a bored look.

14

Oompa Lumpa

'Jess,' called Dad. 'Time to get up.'

'Oomf yert,' I called back. Strange. I couldn't move my face and I could hardly open my eyes or mouth. I stumbled out of bed and went to the bathroom. Something was stuck to the back of my legs. My bed sheet! I peeled it off and dropped it on the floor. How did that happen? Wax. There must have been some left on my legs from yesterday and it had acted like glue. Yuk. I tried again to open my eyes properly. 'Warghhhh!' A ghoul with bloodshot eyes stared back at me and . . . Oh. My. God. It was me! What had happened to my eyebrows? They were blacker than black. Oh no. I'd forgotten to take the tint off them when I'd wiped my eyelashes. It had been on all night. Too dark, too dark! My eyes were slits, swollen and red. I must have had an allergic reaction to the tint – probably because I left it on so long, not the five minutes max it said on the bottle. It must have soaked right into my eye sockets. I ran hot water and splashed my face to wipe off the face mask. It wasn't budging. It had set like concrete. Freaky. It looked like a death mask. I set about dabbing hot water onto my cheeks, and little by little, the mask turned into a paste and finally washed off. Phew. I looked back in the mirror. Nooooooooooooooooooooo! My face was bright orange, I mean *bright* orange! I ran back to the spray can and peered at the instructions. One coat which will *develop* over six to eight hours! Hadn't Pia read this? I'd put on three coats! I looked at my body. Streaks everywhere and my ankles and wrists were the worst.

'Jess, come on,' called Dad from the hallway outside my room.

'Coming. Just a few minutes,' I called back. I had to wash the oil out of my hair and get the orange colour off quick. I lathered up shampoo but because I was in a rush, some of it got in my eyes making them sting more than ever. 'Arghhhhhh,' I cried as I rinsed off and then scrubbed at my face and body. 'No!' It wasn't working. The orange colour had soaked into my skin like sepia ink. I stepped out of the shower and got my hairdryer. *Pale make-up*, I thought as I blow-dried, *that will disguise my skin*. When my hair was dry, I plastered on some foundation. I sat back to survey the result. Disaster with a capital D. My hair looked lank and greasy and, what was worse, it stank like chip fat. My eyebrows stood out like two angry gashes above my puffy eyes. My skin glowed orange underneath the foundation. I looked like a clown.

'The door opened behind me. 'Dad says—' Charlie started then burst out laughing. 'What happened to you?'

'DIY beauty session,' I wailed.

'Christ!'

'Is it really that bad?'

'Worse. What do you think?'

I burst into tears. 'What am I going to do? I can't go into school looking like this.'

'No. Blimey.' Charlie stared at me. 'When you said you wanted to stand out from the crowd, you didn't have to go this far.'

'Not funny.'

Dad appeared at the door and his face dropped. 'Jess! What happened? What have you done to yourself?'

I pointed at the can and beauty products that were now on my dressing table. 'Spray tan and I think I left eyebrow tint on too long.'

Dad's face began to crack. He glanced at Charlie who was also having a hard time not laughing.

'Don't! Either of you. Help me. What am I going to do?'

Dad came over and took a close look at my face. 'Your eyes are rather swollen but . . . you can see all right, can't you?'

'Ish. Yes.'

'The swelling will go down. Have you splashed cold water?'

I nodded.

'Have you tried the shower for the . . . the er suntan?'

'It doesn't touch it.'

Dad looked at his watch. 'Heavens. I have to be at my desk and you have to get to school.'

'No way. I can't go in like this. I can't let anyone see me.'

'Do you feel ill?' asked Dad.

'No.'

'Then you go to school.'

'But . . .'

'No buts,' said Dad. 'Now get a move on.'

'That's so not fair. You don't understand,' I groaned but Dad had gone. So much for me thinking being selected for the modelling contest would bring me kudos. I'd be the laughing stock.

Dad reappeared. 'Wanda Carlsen. Go and see Pia's mum. Quick.'

At that moment the phone rang. Charlie went to answer. He came back sniggering. 'It's Pia. She's got an oompa lumpa face as well.'

I grabbed the phone. 'Can your mum help?' I asked.

'She says get over here right away. I am so grounded after this but she thinks she can do something.'

I grabbed my coat and a hat which I pulled way down my face and put on the biggest pair of sunglasses I could find, flew out the door and over to Pia's. She opened the door looking almost as orange as I did. She burst out laughing when she saw me.

'Not you too, Pia. This is so not funny.'

'Now I'm as *special* as you,' she said with a big grin. She didn't seem as bothered as I was but then she wasn't a contestant in a modelling competition.

Mrs Carlsen was hovering behind. 'Come in, Jess, and get upstairs. Honestly. The pair of you should be shot. What were you thinking? Don't you realise that spray tan needs to be applied correctly and it takes time to develop.'

'Someone didn't read the instructions,' I said as I took the stairs two by two.

'I thought you had,' said Pia.

'I thought *you* had and at least you don't have slits for eyes.'

'Don't worry,' said Mrs Carlsen when we reached the bathroom. 'What you need is exfoliator. I've mixed one that'll take the top layer off. Lemon and baking soda. We haven't got time to do you all over now so make a start on your faces and you can do the rest of you this evening when you get back from school.'

We stood over the sink and scrubbed away with the lotion she brought us. Thankfully some of the orange did seem to be coming off but not all of it, plus my face and skin were bright red and sore from the scrubbing.

After another scrub, I heard Charlie's voice shouting through the letterbox. 'Come on, Jess. Dad says you've got to come or we'll miss our bus.'

There was nothing else for it. I had to go. I dashed home, put on my uniform, slapped on some more pale foundation which, with the black eyebrows, made me look like a kid who'd had their face painted. 'Arghhhh.'

'Come on, Jess,' called Charlie.

'Have we got a balaclava anywhere?' I called back as I wiped the foundation off.

'Nope. And anyway, you wouldn't be able to wear it all day.'

I raced down the stairs where Pia was waiting with Charlie.

'We'll be orange and proud,' she said as we ran for the gate and out to the bus stop.

'Yeah right,' I said. 'Just as long as we don't bump into Tom. Oh God. I want to hide under my duvet.'

'We'll sort it,' said Pia. 'We'll have another scrub sesh tonight.'

'Will I look normal for Saturday? It's round three of the competition.'

'Mum will think of something,' she said.

Luckily we caught our bus and I got out my small mirror to see how bad I looked. My eyelids were still swollen and it looked like I'd been crying for a week.

Oh God. I so wished I didn't have to go into school. I was dreading it.

As soon as we got off the bus, I put my head down, collar up and headed inside.

'Hey, Hall, how's it going in the model world?' said a male voice behind me. I knew it was Tom. Blooming Murphy's law. I go days without seeing him and the one day I don't want to see him, he's the first person I bump into.

'Great, great,' I said as I hurried on. 'Can't stop. Am late, late, go to go.'

'Too good for me now, eh?' he asked as he ran to catch me up, pranced in front of me then stopped and whistled. 'Wow! What happened to you?

'Captured by aliens last night. Alert the planet that they've landed. Try to save yourself. Pia and I are still suffering from the radiation. Don't come too near.'

Tom cracked up. 'Seriously. What happened?'

'I just told you. Aliens. They've taken over Pia's brain already.'

Pia nodded. 'Beoink a zatta goinosh,' she said then went into what I guess she imagined was an alien walk but looked more like she'd stuck her hand in an electric socket.

Tom shook his head. 'I always knew you were different, Hall. That's why I like you and your strange friend.'

'Me and a long list of girls,' I replied. 'I know what you're like.'

'Ah yes. But can I help it if I'm irresistible?' He smiled his killer-watt smile which, I had to admit, was pretty irresistible.

'You're so arrogant,' I said.

He bowed. 'Thanks. I try to be. Oh and Hall, I hear that the last round of the modelling show is open to the public. The catwalk show. Any chance you can get me a ticket?'

'Get your own,' Pia piped up. 'You only want to go because you know there'll be loads of gorgeous girls there.'

'Oh, so she's got her brain back for a moment,' said Tom. 'And actually no, I thought I'd come along and cheer you all on.'

'That's if either of us gets through. Somehow, I don't think having a face like a boiled tomato is going to be what the judges are looking for.'

'Maybe they're vegetarians. You might be just what they want.'

We'd reached the hall. As pupils streamed past us, a few glanced over then did a double take.

'Aliens have landed,' said Pia. 'Beware of radiation. Fight for your life. Don't look at us. It's catching. Save yourselves.'

'Nutters,' said Josh Tyler as he joined Tom and pulled him into assembly.

I trooped in after them. By now, loads of people were staring and pointing. It was going to be a crap day.

After school, it was straight back to Pia's for another go with the lemon and baking soda. It took a little more of the colour off and Mrs Carlsen also had some tint remover which brought my eyebrows back to a more normal colour. When I was ready to go, she gave me a bottle of her exfoliator. 'Twice a day for the next week,' she said. 'You should be OK, maybe glowing a little on Saturday but you won't look like you've overdone it too much.'

I thanked her and headed for home where I found Charlie at the breakfast bar eating one of his enormous peanut butter sandwiches.

'Mff,' he said through a mouthful.

I nodded back. 'Mff.'

I made myself a jam and peanut sandwich and sat down to join him. I was starving. I'd had no lunch because I didn't want to go in the dining room and be stared at. Instead, Pia and I had gone to the library and hidden. She'd also got fed up with the attention by midday as even the teachers had been having a laugh at our expense.

'Sheila had to go early. She's left some lasagna.'

'Mff,' I said.

We continued eating in silence for a while. I wasn't in the mood for conversation.

'You look better,' Charlie said when he'd finished. 'And the swelling on your eyes has gone down.'

I nodded. Charlie got up, started to go towards the stairs then came back and stood looking at his feet. 'Er . . .'

'What?'

He turned to go again. 'Nothing.' He turned back.

'What?'

'Flo.'

'What about her?'

'Er . . . do you think she still likes me?'

'Like like or *like* like?'

'*Like* like.'

'Why are you interested all of a sudden?'

Charlie shrugged. 'Dunno.'

I wasn't going to tell him that she'd been interested since she was about nine. She had a photo of him by her pillow. She regularly looked at his Facebook, read all his lyrics, listened to any new song he posted on there in the hope that one day he might write a song about her.

'Well, something must have changed. Up until now, you ran a mile if she as much as looked at you. Is it because she's got someone else now?'

'No. Yes. OK. Truth. I was watching her the other day when we were doing your modelling shots and it was like . . . like I saw her for the first time and saw . . .'

'How lovely she is.'

Charlie hesitated for a few moments. 'Yes. She is. Sweet too. Is it too late?'

'Probably. She's pretty thick with Alexei.'

Charlie sighed heavily. 'And I guess I could never compete with someone like that.'

'What do you mean? Someone like that?'

He pointed up at the ceiling. 'Someone who lives upstairs and is loaded. Even as a bloke, I can see he's good-looking. He's got it all, yeah?'

'I guess, but you're good-looking and talented. Maybe not rich but you've got a lot going for you, I can see that even if you are my brother.' I knew exactly what he was saying though. It was how I felt about JJ. Was he, and always would be, in a different league to me? All I knew was that I had to be cool with him. He'd sent me texts every other day with bits of news but I'd only replied to one as I was hoping I could keep him interested by not being so available. Charlie looked so dejected, I had to say something. *What would Mum say?* I asked myself.

'Go for it, Chaz,' I said. 'If you like Flo, tell her. Sometimes you have to fight for what you want. Don't give in before it's even started. Only Flo knows what she feels for you and what she feels for Alexei. I know what Mum would say. She'd say that if a person is the right one, then it doesn't matter what their background is or how rich or poor they are and if it does matter to them, then they're not worth knowing.'

Charlie smiled sadly. 'She would have said that, wouldn't she?'

I nodded. 'Hey, do you think Dad ever feels like this? You know, us and them? All day he has to run around serving the residents' every need. We've both seen it. Some of them are so polite and lovely but I've seen some of them order him around like he's one of their servants.'

'I don't know. I've never asked him.'

'I wonder if he fancies any of the residents and thinks, no way am I in with a chance?'

'It's different for him. He's general manager. He couldn't get involved with any of the residents because of his position, even if he wanted to.'

'I thought he and Tanisha would make a nice couple but she's got a boyfriend.'

Charlie smiled. 'Matchmaker. Actually, I wondered if he might like Pia's mum.'

'Me too! For about a nanosecond. She's way too bossy for him. She's already telling him how to the run the place and driving him mad. Pia told me.'

'I wonder if he'd like a girlfriend.'

'Probably hasn't got time.'

After Charlie had gone up to play his music, I had a good think about what we'd talked about. Were Dad, Charlie and I to be cursed with a lack of self-worth just because we lived in Porchester Park and weren't as rich as the residents? I never felt like this before I moved here, that was for sure. Was it a case of us and them as far as relationships went? And we should stick to people more like us? It didn't seem to bother Flo or at least she hadn't talked about it. I made a resolution to ask her about Alexei next time I got her alone. My thoughts drifted back to Tom. He'd been flirty today even when I was looking my worst, and as always, there was a spark between us that I couldn't deny. Was that because I felt more of an equal with him? *I mustn't think about him*, I told myself. *Tom's a player. JJ's the type who wouldn't mess me around but then if I did go out with him, would time reveal that he lives in another world to me, a world I could never be a part of?*

Go for it. I heard Mum's voice in my head saying similar words to the ones I'd just spoken to Charlie. *Tell him how you feel. Don't be afraid of being rejected. The right one will like you, love you, just the way you are. Don't be afraid or give in to self-doubt.*

So that I didn't get into worrying about it all again, I decided to put on a CD to drown out my thoughts. One of Mum's old favourites was already in the player. Elton John. 'Don't go changing, trying to please me, I love you just the way you are.'

Spooky, I thought as I put the lasagna in the microwave to heat up.

15

Round Three

'I see I wasn't the only one who's been beautifying up,' I said to Flo as we filtered into the building where round three of the modelling competition was to take place.

She looked at the other girls. 'I guess everyone wants to win,' she observed.

It felt strange to be there with a smaller number of us plus a couple of parents or elder sisters hanging around. A few girls had had spray tans although it looked like they'd had it done professionally. I was the only one who had gone for the streaky bacon look. Most girls were wearing skintight clothes, jeans and little T-shirts to show off their figures. Flo and I had come bundled up in scarves and jackets because although it was March, the weather still felt wintery. One girl had had her hair cut, another straightened, even Flo'd had eyelashes extensions. I thought they look odd on her, like big spiders stuck on her eyes. Keira arrived just after us. She looked striking, all in black as usual, the only colour was a gash of bright red lipstick. She glanced over, then, as everyone had this last week, did a double take. I took a sharp intake of breath to prepare myself for some nasty comment as she came over.

'Spray tan disaster?' she asked.

I nodded.

'I did the same thing once. Poor you. Bad timing with the competition and all.'

'Er . . . yeah.'

'Have you tried exfoliator? Anything with lemon in, it acts as bleach.'

'Yes and baking soda.' *What was going on?* I wondered. Keira offering me advice?

'So how's it going?' she said, cosying in for a friendly chat.

'Er . . . good, well actually not so good I guess, being orange and all.'

Keira pulled me to one side. 'It'll fade. Look, I'm sorry we got off on the wrong foot. I'd . . . I'd been feeling depressed, the move back to the UK really got to me and I took it out on you. I'm sorry I dissed you. Can we start again? No hard feelings? Turn the page? Move on?'

'I . . . yes of course,' I said, although I wasn't sure and a warning bell rang inside. I'd been hurt by what she'd said and how she'd acted but then she had apologised and didn't everyone deserve a second chance? It would be mean of me to shut her out.

Keira squeezed my arm. 'Great,' she said. 'So. Ready for today?'

'Ish.'

'Well, good luck and . . . I mean that.'

'You too,' I replied.

The rest of the day was like living out a fantasy. We were each given our own make-up artist to get us ready for our head shots. Mine was a petite blonde girl called Chloe. She didn't look much older than me.

'A miracle,' I said after she'd applied skin colour so perfect that by the time she'd finished, I looked sun-kissed and healthy as opposed to a freak.

'We can disguise most anything,' she said. 'At college, we did film make-up and I can make anyone look like a model or a monster.'

'Model today, please,' I said. 'I've done the monster look.'

Suzie passed around the room watching what was happening. 'Keep it natural, guys,' she said. 'Next week we'll up the glamour for the catwalk, today we want casual so no heavy make-up.'

I closed my eyes and left Chloe to it. It felt like she was putting loads on as she brushed, rubbed and stroked but when I opened my eyes, it was fab. I had my Sunday best look at last.

After make-up, it was time for the shots. Each of us had to wait our turn to be taken into the room where the photographer had set up. Keira was called first. As I sat waiting with Flo, it gave us a good chance to look at the other girls in the competition.

Flo glanced at a tall, willowy girl with Titian red long hair. 'She's my favourite to win,' she said. 'She looks like a Pre-Raphaelite princess. Who do *you* think will win?'

I looked over at the contestants. There were two stunning black girls. One with short hair and amazing high cheekbones and a strong athletic body, the other had long hair like silk and could have been Naomi Campbell's younger sister. Chatting to them was a stunning curvy Indian girl who also had long black hair and big brown doe eyes. 'Maybe Nita,' I said. 'I reckon she could play a goddess in a Bollywood film, she's so perfect.'

'I guess it depends on what the judges are looking for though, doesn't it?' said Flo.

'Not after today,' I said. 'After five o'clock, it's over to the public for the final choice. I reckon it will depend on who has the most friends.'

'Or who's good at using the Net,' said Flo. 'If we're serious, we should get everyone on Facebook to ask their friends to ask their friends to ask their friends and so on.'

'You do realise that our votes will be halved then because we know all the same people, go to the same school,' I said.

Flo shrugged. 'Maybe they could vote twice!'

'I think Misaki's in with a good chance too,' I said as we watched a beautiful Japanese girl, who was near to us, apply kohl to her eyes. 'She's got her own look.'

Flo nodded. 'She does stand out,' she agreed. Misaki dressed like a Victorian waif with strong dark make-up and her hair piled high on her head. Her dress sense reminded me of Riko Mori, a teenage girl whose family had an apartment at Porchester Park. She was away at school so I rarely saw her but when she was home, she dressed in an eccentric style all of her own. She wasn't as friendly as Misaki was either – unlike some of the other contestants, Misaki always had a ready smile and was happy to chat while we were waiting about.

'God, they're all gorgeous,' I said. 'The blonde girls still in the competition are stunning too and both so different.' One was stick thin with a boy's figure and an elfin face, the other was a Barbie lookalike, a picture of health with thick golden hair and a radiant wide smile which showed whiter than white perfect teeth.

'I feel so bland next to them,' I said.

'Me too,' said Flo.

'You're not bland,' I said. 'There's no-one else like you in the competition. You're our token romantic.' With her big grey dreamy eyes, Flo was the perfect English rose.

'What do you think of Keira's chances?' I asked.

Flo shrugged. 'She's striking, no doubt about that, but there's a hardness in her eyes which could work for some shots but not for others. I reckon she'll lose out on votes though as she doesn't know that many people over here.'

'Maybe, but people don't have to live in the UK to vote. Once it goes onto the Net, she could get her Australian mates to vote.'

'Keira doesn't strike me as the kind of girl who has a lot of mates,' said Flo. 'She's not a girl's girl.'

I glanced at the other brunette besides me in the competition. Like the others, she was very pretty with shoulder-length layered hair. 'God, I don't know what I'm doing here.'

'Stop being so down on yourself, Jess. You're as good-looking as the rest of them.'

'But bland. I think I look ordinary.'

'Ah but that's what works sometimes. Not that you're ordinary, I didn't mean that, but to be a model, you have to be versatile, be able to do a whole range of looks. Sometimes they need a face that's a blank canvas but can be made to look glamorous or sporty. Like Misaki, she's got such a strong look but that might be her only look.'

'Maybe. It's a shame we can't all go in the room for the shots together. I'd like to have watched everyone and see what they do.'

'Me too,' said Flo. 'I find it hard when anyone points a camera and says smile. I always look so false.'

'Think of something funny or someone you fancy,' I said. 'Think of Alexei or . . . Charlie.'

'If I thought about Charlie I'd probably look cross,' said Flo. 'Or like I wanted to kill someone!'

'Why?'

'Oh, you know.'

'Do you still like him?'

'After a five-year crush, what do you think? But we both know he's not interested.'

'Ah but do we? What about Alexei? I thought it was love and Charlie was history.'

Flo shrugged. 'Alexei's great but . . .'

'What?'

'I don't know. Something's missing, like when we kiss. Not that I've kissed many boys but the ones I have kissed, it felt like they were with me, they come forward and it's a mutual thing. I feel with Alexei that he's . . . oh I don't know. I guess what I'm trying to say is that there's no real chemistry. I don't feel anything – so maybe it's me not him. I like him, but love? No. Not this time.'

'So what are you going to do?'

'I've been putting off telling him. I don't want to hurt his feelings and I know he's lonely. He doesn't know many people here in London.'

'But if you're not into him, you have to tell him.'

Flo nodded. 'I know. I will.'

'You can still hang out, be friends.'

'I hope so. I do like him. I reckon we'd be good friends. He's sweet and it's been fun hanging out at his apartment.'

'How do you feel about that? Do you ever feel like you're not good enough?

'How?'

'Like not rich enough?'

Flo looked surprised. 'God no. I don't think stuff like that matters if you like each other. Would you look down on someone who wasn't as well off as you?'

'Oh. I don't think so. No. I never even think about stuff like that. I either like someone or not.'

'So why should Alexei or any of them at Porchester Park be any different? Not if they're nice people. My gran says someone can only make you feel inferior if you give them permission. I think I know what she means, like the problem's in you, not them.'

Suzie appeared at the door. 'Jessica Hall. You're next.'

I got up to go. Flo gave me the thumbs up. 'Just relax. And you think of Tom or JJ,' she said with a smile.

'I will,' I said. 'And . . . about Charlie.'

'What about him?'

'I think he may have just woken up to you,' I said.

Flo's face lit up. 'Really? Has he said something?'

'Come on, Jessica,' urged Suzie.

I followed her into a room that had been set up with cameras, lights and a plain backdrop. Derek was standing at the back with a camera.

'Oh, it's you!' I said.

He nodded. 'Yep, and I can tell you I prefer doing this to being a judge. So, come on in and stand in the centre over there.'

I went to the spot he'd indicated. It was hard to see because the lights were so bright.

'OK, relax,' said Derek. 'Shoulders down. I'm not going to bite, well, only a little. Now, look into the camera, tilt your head, that's it.' He immediately started to fire off shots then suddenly stopped. 'No, no. You looked like someone's just pinched your bum. Relax. You're too stiff. What's your name again?'

'Jess.'

'OK, Jess. Let's go again. Head right, head left.

Chin up, chin down, that's it. Stick your tongue out. Pout. Sneer at me. Smile at me. Flirt with the camera. Get into it. Give me as many different expressions as you can. We only need a couple of shots. Forget about me, pretend you're in an acting class and the brief is for twenty expressions in twenty seconds. Go for it.'

I did my best and tried to think about different things, starting with JJ.

'Good, good, better,' said Derek.

I kept trying to focus on JJ but Tom's image kept coming in. Tom flirting, Tom prancing in front of me, some of the things he'd said, the first time we'd kissed. *Get out of my mind, Tom Robertson*, I thought. *Out, out, out.*

'No, no, no, NO,' said Derek from behind his camera. 'You've lost it. You look worried, too anxious. I said happy thoughts! What on earth were you thinking about?'

'Oh, er just someone.'

'A boy?'

I nodded.

'You like him?'

'No. OK, maybe, yes. I don't know.'

'He's trouble?'

'A player.'

'Ah. He's cute?'

'And some. He knows it too. He's so full of himself.'

OK,' said Derek. 'Let's try this then, imagine him in the most droopy unflattering pair of Y-fronts, nothing else, his knees are knocked, his legs skinny and a bird just pooed right on his perfect head.'

I burst out laughing and Derek fired a shot. 'Got it, Jess. Great.' He fired a few more rounds. 'Right. Now let's go for a more moody shot. Think about something sad.'

No problem there. I thought about my mum. How she would have loved to have been here. How she'd have loved hearing about every small detail of the competition. She was so brave in the last months before she died. The only time she cried was when we talked about my future and she realised all the times she was going to miss. Times like this.

'Wow,' said Derek. 'You can do sad all right, Jess. Hope it's not about the same boy.'

I shook my head. 'No.'

'Don't want to talk about it?'

I shook my head again.

'We'll move on,' said Derek. 'Now let's have some fun. Think about something mad. No. Pretend someone's doing something mad right next to you and you're watching. Go.'

No problem there either. I thought about Pia. Pia pretending to be an alien at school, telling people to save themselves when we were bright orange. Pia attempting to dry my dad's duvet with a hairdryer once when Dave had weed on it. Lying on the floor, laughing as Dave sat smugly on the bed. Derek moved around me shooting.

'Excellent,' he said. 'Now we're cooking. Once more to camera. OK. Jess, you're done.'

That wasn't so bad, I thought as I headed out the door. I liked Derek. He had a fatherly quality and made it easy by talking and telling me what to do and think.

Once everyone had done their close-up, we were told to go out for an hour and grab some lunch while the judges decided who were the final ten. Flo and I headed off to a café down the road where we bought soup and a roll. Flo called Meg and I called Pia to fill them in on the morning's events. My phone had another message from JJ.

Look forward to seeing you in over a week. XX.

Part of me wanted to text him back but I didn't because I still wanted to maintain that I was cool and not appear too easy. He was probably having a great time where he was, surrounded by rich, gorgeous girls and not missing me at all.

When we got back to Atlas Buildings after lunch, there was the usual tense atmosphere as waited for the results. Misaki told us that Tanisha had arrived while we were out and it wasn't long before she came through with the judges.

'Oh, with the long faces,' she said when she saw us all sitting there in silence. 'I know it's hard but as I said last time, it's good practice for if you really do ever go into modelling. It's a competitive world and you have to be tough to take the knocks so it's best to find out now if you've got what it takes.'

Derek motioned to a young man at the back who was standing behind a projector. 'Let's see how you all did this morning, hey? I bet you're all dying to see how everyone did.'

Moments later, a slideshow of our shots played onto a screen. Some of them were fabulous and I could see so clearly that some girls were so much more photogenic than others. Some girls who looked stunning in the flesh didn't look so good in their shots and others who weren't quite as stunning looked amazing in their photos. Keira looked fantastic, broody and sultry, looking straight into camera through half-closed eyes. Flo's weren't so great. She looked like she didn't want to be there never mind have her photo taken. Misaki's were brilliant. In some, she looked like she had real attitude, in others, she looked soft and vulnerable. Suddenly mine flashed up.

'Wow,' Flo whispered when the first shot flashed up. 'That's fantastic. You'll definitely get through.'

It took me a moment to recognise myself and when I did, I had to admit, it was a great shot. It was the photo that Derek had taken when I was thinking about how Pia makes me laugh and I looked relaxed and totally at ease.

'It's going to be hard for the judges and the public. Everyone looks great,' I said.

After we'd seen the results of Derek's work, we were asked to line up.

'I'm not going to get through,' Flo whispered.

I squeezed her hand. 'Course you are.'

'No, I don't mind. I've had it with these line-ups. I always want to laugh when it gets tense.'

'Me too.'

Once more the judges stared at us and we stared back. After what seemed an eternity, five girls were asked to step forward. Flo was one of them. Keira and Misaki were left in the line behind with me.

'I am sorry, girls, but you won't be going any further this time,' said Tanisha. When she saw that some of them were in tears, she went and gave them a hug and had an individual chat with them.

The line with me realised that we'd got through and in an instant, there were hugs and tears and jumping up and down. I felt strangely removed from it all. I was through. Keira was through. 'Congratulations,' she said and gave me a hug.

'Oh. Yes. You too,' I said. I looked over at Flo. She gave me the thumbs up and grinned.

'Sorry about your friend,' said Keira then went off to air-kiss the skinny blonde girl who'd got through. Flo came over to join me.

'I don't mind that I'm out, honestly,' she said as she put on her jacket to go. 'I knew my shots didn't go well today.'

'I'm so sorry,' I said and gave her a hug. 'It won't be the same without you. It seems wrong that I'm in and you're not.'

Flo shook her head. 'Modelling's not for me, Jess. I don't want to spend all my time worrying about what I eat and how my skin is. I feel like I've spent the last few weeks obsessing about how I look and, to tell the truth, I haven't really enjoyed it, like everyone's looking at each other, sizing each other up, it's so competitive. I didn't like being judged and told I have to find a look and that line-up was so tense! I was happy before. I'm looking forward to getting back to being normal.'

I nodded. I knew what she meant about obsessing. I didn't like it either. It felt like there were more important things to think about than how my bum looked in the mirror and I still didn't like that so many girls were excluded for not being the right shape or look.

'I'll wait for you outside,' said Flo with a quick glance at Keira. 'Just in case you need any support later.'

I gave her another hug. She was a good mate.

After the eliminations, the ten girls that were left had to pose for a full-length group shot. We were given pink tracksuits with **Teen Queen** emblazoned on the front in silver glitter.

'Big smiles,' Derek directed. 'You're a fun group, you're the girls everyone wants to be with. Now let me have it! Give me a leap into the air and shout yay like you just got your exam results and got A stars all the way!'

'Yay,' we chorused as we jumped.

'These will go up on the web tomorrow and the public can start voting,' said Suzie once Derek had finished and everyone was gathering their things to go. 'Good luck, have a good week, plenty of sleep and I'll see you all next week for dress fittings.'

It's been a good day, I thought as I made my way out the building with the others. I was so pleased that Keira and I were cool with each other now. I hated not getting on with people.

Flo was waiting for me outside and we headed off to meet Aunt Maddie who'd texted that she'd be waiting for me in the café opposite. I quickly filled Flo in on what she'd missed.

'Derek's fab, isn't he?' she said.

'And Keira was so nice.'

Flo frowned. 'I'd watch out if I were you, Jess. Keep your friends close and your enemies even closer. Ever heard that line? That's what Keira's doing I reckon. All she cares about is winning the competition. Don't trust her.'

'No honestly, I think she was on the level. Today really made me think. Like one day, you think life is rubbish and it's never going to get better, ever again, then you have a day like today, a sunny day. I'm going to remember this feeling. Everything changes, everything passes.'

Flo bowed and said in a Yoda from *Star Wars* voice, 'Wise you have grown, little one. Into the world soon I can let you go.'

I laughed.

'I'm glad you had a good time, Jess, but . . . just don't let Keira get too close to you. You might trust her but I don't.'

'Nah. She's cool. I really think our bad days are behind us. History.'

Aunt Maddie had already ordered hot chocolates for us, and as we sat in the warm café, I looked out of the window.

'You look happy,' said Aunt Maddie.

'I am,' I said. 'It's been fun today.' As I stared out of the window, I saw Keira come out of the building where we'd just been. She waved at someone over the road, smiled and began to cross. I moved over slightly so that I could see who she'd seen just in time to see a tall boy with shoulder-length brown hair wrap his arms around her then kiss her. It would have been a wonderfully romantic moment to have witnessed . . . if only the boy hadn't been Tom.

16

Who, What, Where, When, How?

'How?' I gasped.

'When?' asked Flo.

'Who?' asked Aunt Maddie.

'*Why?*' I could hardly believe my eyes. History was repeating itself. So that was why Keira was being so chummy today. She knew she was seeing Tom later. My head was spinning. I felt as if I'd been punched in the stomach. Even I was surprised at how upset I felt. *He's not even yours*, I told myself.

'What—' Aunt Maddie started when the café door opened and Pia and Meg rushed over to join us.

'You saw?' asked Flo.

They both nodded. 'You OK?' asked Pia.

'Is anyone going to tell me what's going on?' Aunt Maddie demanded.

Pia looked at me. I looked at Flo. Flo looked at Meg. Aunt Maddie looked at all of us. 'I'm waiting.'

'Boys, Aunt Maddie,' I said. 'They do your head in.'

'Ah. And which boy is this?' she asked. 'I thought you liked the one at Porchester Park. Isn't he away?'

'Er, we'll go and get more supplies,' said Pia and she dragged Meg off to the counter with her.

'I'll come and help,' said Flo.

Aunt Maddie was still waiting for my answer. 'You mean JJ. I do like him. It's still early days with us but he has promised to take me on a date when he's back. Thing is . . . I don't know if it could ever work with us. You know how it is, Aunt M, his family are loaded, they travel in a private jet, holiday on exclusive islands, have credit cards falling out of their pockets. I can't hope to keep up. I'm pretty sure it won't work.'

Aunt Maddie glanced out of the window. 'So who did you just see?'

'Tom Robertson. I've had a crush on him since he arrived at our school at the end of last year. That's not easy either though.'

'Tell me.'

I sighed. 'He goes to my school. He's arrogant, he's full of himself, just about every girl at school is in love with him, me included. There I've said it. We do have chemistry. Least I thought we did. I'm careful not to let him know that I'm into him though. He's the kind of boy who likes a challenge.'

'You're not a girl afraid of a challenge so why not go for him?'

'I've been trying to play it cool because there are so many girls into him.'

'Which boy do you like best?'

'That's what's so difficult. I like both of them, for different reasons. Tom's a laugh but he's not into having a proper relationship. He's the biggest flirt on the planet. JJ's so interesting and good to talk to but I can't help but think that he's out of my league and it wouldn't work with him so I can't let my head get too into thinking about him. I suppose I was keeping my options open in case either of them let me down or if anything happened like just now when I saw Tom snogging Keira!' I pointed out of the window. 'That's who we just saw.'

'Ah. I get the picture. You OK?'

I don't know anything any more, I thought. 'One minute sunshine, next minute rain. See, Aunt M, I thought if I went in for this modelling competition, Tom would be more interested in me. I wouldn't be little Miss Ordinary any more. I'd stand out from everyone else on his list of devotees at school. And I thought JJ might not think of me as way beneath him as well.'

Aunt Maddie whistled through her teeth. 'Phew. I don't envy you being a teenager these days. I don't get it though. I really don't. Do you really think that all the other girls at your school are ordinary? Or that you're ordinary? I'd call you normal not ordinary. There's a difference.'

'Normal? That's not a word I can even relate to these days.' I hoped that she wasn't going to go into one of her lectures. I so wasn't in the mood.

'I don't know, Jess. It seems that things have got a bit lopsided in your world and when it comes to the heart, sometimes you have to take a risk. Do either of the boys know how you really feel?'

'No way. With Tom I might end up on a list of rejects and with JJ, he might soon get bored when he realises I can't keep up with his lifestyle.'

Aunt Maddie nodded. 'So you've taken the safe option to protect yourself by not choosing either.

But not being brave enough to open up and make yourself vulnerable hasn't made you any happier, has it?'

Oh, here we go, I thought. 'Understatement. I don't know what I'm doing any more. I don't know who I am any more and I don't know what I want. If you can call that lopsided, then you're right.'

'No need to get tetchy, Jess. I just think you need to make up your mind who you want and go for it. Don't be afraid to put yourself into the firing line and fight for someone when the heart is concerned.' *Maybe she's right, maybe I should have replied to some of JJ's texts*, I thought. *Oh I don't know!*

Luckily, Meg, Flo and Pia reappeared and Aunt Maddie dropped the lecture.

'OK,' said Pia. 'So you forget about Tom, yeah? He's a loser.'

'Forget about Tom? Easy to say.'

Pia ignored my comment, made a gesture with her hand as if brushing it away, then she produced a piece of paper. 'Tom's not the priority this week. Me and the girls were chatting in the queue for drinks. We've decided, you have to be like a footballer before a match. No distractions. Focus on the game. I've made a list. You jog, you drink water with lemon in it, lots of it – *so* good for your skin – you get lots of sleep, you eat raw food, you condition your hair.'

Flo and I exchanged glances.

Aunt Maddie laughed. 'Your love life might be complicated, Jess, but at least you have good friends.'

'I mean it,' said Pia. 'Flo said your shots today were great. We think you could win.'

'The photos go live on the site tomorrow and then it's down to votes,' said Flo.

'Let me take care of that,' said Meg. 'My brother's a whiz on computers. We'll get you votes.'

'All the other girls will have brothers too,' I said.

Pia made an exaggerated miserable face. 'And that attitude has to go too!'

She can be a bossy cow at times. Does no-one realise that my heart has just been broken?

The rest of the week, Pia was true to her word. She got me up at seven and out jogging.

At break in school, she made me drink so much water, I had to ask for permission in class to go to the loo. Twice.

She stood over me as I applied her mum's rejuvenating skin cream.

She talked her mum into giving me the proper pro all-over spray tan job. I looked like I'd been for a few weeks in the Caribbean when she'd finished.

On Thursday, I had to go to Atlas Buildings for a fitting for my casual outfit and my evening dress for the catwalk finale and Pia came with me. A whole rail of clothes had been loaned by designers wanting PR for their collections. Suzie had already picked out who should wear what. My casual outfit was OK, nothing spectacular but then none of them were – just jeans and various sporty tops. My dress was gorgeous though. An off-the-shoulder, peacock blue silk number by Mercedes Valanti, an up-and-coming new designer. I felt like a star when I had it on.

'It looks fantastic,' said Pia. 'It brings out your eyes and looks great with your hair colour.'

I noticed Keira at the other side of the room getting into a flame red dress. It looked stunning. I also noticed that she wasn't being so friendly today.

'Go and ask her about Tom,' said Pia.

I shook my head. 'She'll only realise that I cared, although I am curious as to how they met.'

'Coward,' said Pia.

She was right. 'Put yourself in the firing line,' Aunt Maddie had said. She was right too. I'd been pussyfooting around for long enough as far as boys were concerned. I took a deep breath and went over. 'Great dress, Keira.'

She shrugged. 'Not sure red is my colour but Suzie insists.'

'I . . . so, I saw you with a boy from our school last Saturday.'

She gave me a fake smile. 'Tom. Yeah. I wondered when you were going to ask me about him.'

'How did you two meet?'

'That day I came to see you at your school. After you'd got onto the bus, he saw me and then—'

'Wow. That's weeks ago. Why didn't you say anything?'

'I knew you were into him so I didn't want to freak you out. I saw your journal that day in the café, remember?'

'You looked at my journal?'

'You left it lying on the table. Interesting read.'

'But if you knew I liked him, why did you go out with him?'

'Why not? You aren't a couple, are you? All is fair in love and war, and as far as you and I are concerned, Jess, it's war.'

'Why? What have I ever done to you?'

Keira sized me up. 'Everything always comes so easy to you. In with Tanisha. In with the Lewises. You want JJ but you want Tom as well. Why should you have both of them? You can't have everything and you don't own him just because you have a crush on him and like to write his name in your little book.'

She had me there. He wasn't mine. I knew that only too well. 'Well, just be careful. Tom's a player. There are loads of girls after him.'

'You would say that, wouldn't you? Can't bear for me to have him when you got nowhere with him. Accept it, Jess, he just wasn't that into you.'

Her words cut into me. She was probably right.

Suzie clapped her hands for attention.

'OK, girls, go home, get rest and I'll see you back here on Saturday afternoon ready for the finale,' she said. 'Any questions, problems, give me a call.'

Across the room, Pia was beckoning me away from Keira. She'd obviously seen my face and worked out that the conversation hadn't gone well.

'Hey, don't let her get to you, Jess,' she said when I joined her.

'I'll try not to but . . . I don't understand why she's got it in for me.'

'Because she's jealous, you idiot,' said Pia.

'Why would she be jealous? She's got Tom. She's won.'

Pia rolled her eyes. 'You've got JJ. You've got loads of mates. You're a great person. People like you and are wary of her. Always have been. Listen, Tom does your head in, always has, always will. Boys like that aren't worth the time.'

'So why do I care?'

'Because you're an idiot too,' said Pia. 'But at least you have friends. Come on, let's go. When the going gets tough, the tough go for hot chocolates.'

'Am I allowed, Miss Stricty Pants?'

'Just this once,' she said with a grin.

As we left the building, I noticed Tom hovering at the bottom of the steps.

'Ignore him,' said Pia.

I was about to but then I felt a flash of anger. So he was with Keira now but he'd been playing me along for months. I decided I wasn't going to play any more games. *Are we into each other? Aren't we?* I needed to know the truth. 'Just give me a sec, Pia,' I said and I marched over to Tom.

'Hi, Tom, waiting for Keira?'

He looked uncomfortable then flashed his usual killer-watt smile. 'I might be waiting for you.'

'But you're not, are you? You never told me you knew her when you asked for tickets to the finale.'

He grinned again. 'Ah, I *knew* you cared, Hall.'

This time his arrogant cheek wasn't working its usual charm.

'Yes. I might have cared. Once. But why the secrecy? I've known her for ages and you and me go to the same school. If you've got a girlfriend, why not go public?'

A look of annoyance flashed over his face. 'My private life. I like to keep it private.'

'So that all your other girls don't realise that you're actually with someone? You just want to keep your options open, don't you?'

He sighed heavily and looked at the pavement. 'Keira told me you'd get jealous.'

His words hurt. So they'd been talking about me. Was I jealous? Of course I was but something in me had suddenly changed and it felt like I was seeing clearly for the first time in months.

Tom looked up from the ground. 'We're free agents, Jess. I know we have something special but you know me, I don't do commitment. And I don't have to tell you what I'm doing or answer to you.'

'No. Of course not. Just—'

He sighed again. 'I never took *you* to go all heavy on me.'

'I . . . No. Not heavy, Tom. I didn't mean to come across like that. Just I like things to be clear, I like to know where I stand.'

Tom's eyes twinkled. 'Right here at the bottom of the steps. That's where you stand.'

'Oh haha. Listen. I'm going to be honest. I do like you. Always have and I think you're right we do have something special, could have done anyway, but I don't want to play games or feel I can't say what I want to in case I seem uncool or heavy. I want a boy who plays it straight.'

'I told you that I don't do commitment, Jess.'

'I know. And I think I've finally heard you. Thing is, I do. I'm ready.'

Tom looked worried and put his hand out as if to say, stop. 'Whoa—' he started.

'Not with you, dummy. I get you. You don't do commitment. I heard you this time, loud and clear. But I do. So we're no match. You can cross me off the list. I'm no longer a contender for the Tom Robertson girlfriend wannabe group. I'm moving on to be with someone who actually plays it straight. Someone who doesn't mess with my head and who comes out and says what he wants and feels.'

As I walked away, I felt like a dark cloud that I'd been carrying around for months had lifted. *I've been stupid*, I thought. *Coming up with excuses as to why it won't work with JJ and trying to be cool and aloof, but all along, he's been constant, straight and honest. When you find the right one, you don't have to play head games or try to be someone you're not for fear of losing them.*

As I headed off with Pia, I glanced over at Tom who had now been joined by Keira. She wrapped her arms around him but he was looking over her shoulder after Pia and me and he didn't look happy.

17

Cinderella

'My dress has gone!' I said.

'It can't have,' said Pia. 'Someone's probably moved it.' She began searching through the rails.

It was Saturday afternoon and Pia had come along with me for the final fitting and run-through before the catwalk show in the evening.

'I've looked. It's definitely not there.'

At the other end of the changing room, I saw Keira watching us. My stomach tightened. I knew she had something to do with it.

Suzie appeared behind us. 'What's the problem?' she asked.

'My dress has disappeared.'

Suzie sighed heavily. 'Just what we need.' She glanced at her watch. 'We have an hour. We're supposed to be rehearsing.' She flicked through the rails then picked out a yellow dress with a high neckline and bubble skirt.

'I've sent all the others back. This is the only spare. Put this on.'

'But—'

Suzie's expression showed she wasn't to be argued with and she breezed off to talk to the other girls. I slipped off my jeans and T-shirt and put on the dress. It looked hideous. Yellow makes me look ill, high necklines make my boobs look enormous, the bubble skirt made my knees look knobbly and it didn't fit right at the back.

On the other side of the room, I saw Keira whisper something to the girl with Titian red hair. They both looked over at me and laughed.

'What do you think, P?' I asked.

She shook her head. 'It does nothing for you. You can't appear in that, not after everything you've gone through.'

'So what am I going to do?'

Pia thought for a moment then got out her phone. 'Alisha. I bet she'd lend you any one of her dresses.'

'Oh but I don't feel too happy about asking if I could borrow her clothes. It was one thing when we were doing our DIY fashion shoot because she was there but not now when she's not even in the country.'

'They'll be on their way back from the States by now. I know they're hoping to make the show. I'll see if I can reach her. Come on, she's a mate. You know you'd do the same for her.'

I raced over to Suzie. 'I. . . . If I can get another dress in time, can I wear something else?'

Suzie glanced over me. Even she could see that the yellow dress did me no favours. 'Where are you going to get another couture dress from at this short notice?'

'I have a friend. She has loads of them.'

'Does she now?' Suzie glanced at her watch again. 'You've got just less than two hours. Whilst the others are rehearsing, go and get a dress. Be back at four and if you haven't got a suitable replacement, you wear this one.'

I quickly changed back into my jeans, then as Pia and I headed for the door, Keira came forward and blocked my way. 'Problem?'

'Nothing that can't be sorted,' I said. I was not going to let her win by seeing that she'd ruined things. 'Change of dress, that's all.'

'What a shame,' cooed Keira. 'The blue one looked *so* right.'

I stepped around her. 'Yes, didn't it? Strangely, it seems to have disappeared.'

'Oh really?' said Keira and added with fake concern, 'How *awful* for you.'

'Not at all,' I said. 'I'll find something else.'

'You seem to make a habit of losing things. First Tom, now the dress.'

'You can have Tom,' I said. 'I'm not in the running for him any more but the dress? I think we both know that I didn't lose that.'

Keira tried to do an innocent face. 'Oh, so I wonder what happened to it?'

'So do I. But it doesn't matter, it's only a dress.'

Clearly my reaction wasn't what Keira expected. She thought I'd crumble but I wasn't going to give in that easily.

Pia pulled me away. 'Come on, we've only got two hours.'

Keira laughed. 'Good luck, guys.'

Once outside, Pia looked at her phone and grimaced. 'Alisha's not picking up. It's gone to voicemail. Maybe they're still in the air but they were due to land ages ago.'

'Perhaps their flight was delayed. Charlie's at home. Let's call him and ask if he can get hold of Marguerite and find out what's happening. She'll know what time they're in.'

Pia made the call and explained everything to him. 'He's on the case.'

'But what do we do if they aren't back in time? I can't go up to their apartment if she's not back. I think that would be too cheeky and I already feel uncomfortable about asking her.' I checked my watch. One hour fifty minutes left.

'I agree. Let's call Flo and Meg. Maybe they have something you could borrow?' said Pia and immediately started texting again while I wracked my brains for any other bright ideas.

'Gran!' I said. 'She has a trunkload of clothes from when she was young. Vintage stuff. Remember? We used to dress up in it when we were at junior school.'

'Brill,' said Pia. 'Let's go.'

If we hurried, we could be there in twenty minutes. I already had a dress in mind. A lovely black evening dress with one shoulder strap. Very sophisticated. It used to be too big for me but I'd have grown into it now.

We raced to the bus stop and luckily one came five minutes later. While we were on the bus, Charlie called. As suspected, the Lewises' flight had been delayed – so Alisha and her wonderful wardrobe weren't an option.

Once we reached Hammersmith, we ran to Gran's and banged on the door. The black dress would work, I knew it would. No answer. I banged again. Where was she?

'Oh no! I've just remembered. Gran goes to her art class on a Saturday.'

'Could you phone her?' asked Pia.

'Gran doesn't do mobiles,' I said. I looked at my watch. An hour twenty minutes left. Just at that moment, Gran appeared on the corner of the road. She seemed surprised to see us.

'Phew, thank God,' I said when she reached her front gate. As she let us in, I explained the situation.

Her face fell. 'Oh Jess, I'm so sorry. I gave those clothes to the charity shop months ago. They were just taking up space and you'd grown out of your dressing-up phase.'

So that's it, I thought. *Either I drop out of the competition or I wear the hideous yellow number and look like a plucked chicken.*

'It's not over yet,' said Pia as Gran disappeared into the kitchen to drop her bags. 'If your gran had vintage clothes, so do other people. They sell them to shops. Isn't there a place in Chelsea? There is. Near the tube.'

I knew the place she meant. I glanced at my watch. Would we make it in time? Pia's phone bleeped that she had a message. She looked at her phone then texted back. 'Meg and Flo haven't got anything you could borrow but want to help. They were window shopping in the Kings Road; I've told them to meet us at Sloane Square tube.'

'I'll drive you,' said Gran who had been listening from the open door. 'Come on.'

We hurtled into the car and Gran drove as fast as she could to the shop. Parking was a nightmare, with no spaces anywhere. 'I'll drop you, find somewhere to park then see you at the shop,' she said after we'd driven around the side streets with no luck.

Gran drove back to the shop and we got out. Flo and Meg were already there. They waved as Gran drove off.

'I'm so sorry,' said Flo and pointed at the shop. It was boarded up and there was a sign saying; **Closed for refurbishment. Open again in May.**

'Nooooo,' groaned Pia.

'It's not going to happen,' I said. I glanced at my watch again. Thirty-five minutes to go. If Gran drove us, we'd just about have time to get back to Atlas Buildings. 'God, I hope she's not too long finding somewhere to park.' I looked up at the sky. Clouds were gathering, threatening rain. That would be all I needed. My hair went frizzy in light drizzle. Not a good look for the catwalk and there wouldn't be time, the way things were going, to straighten it.

'Hey,' said Meg and pointed at a shop three doors down. 'Charity shop. Come on. You never know.'

'A charity shop? No way,' I said. 'Who'd ever take a couture dress into a place like that?'

Pia tugged at my arm. 'It's worth a try and this isn't any old area of London. This is Sloane Street. Rich ladies of Kensington territory. I've been into charity shops this end of town before and believe me, you wouldn't believe some of the stuff dropped off. Some of it never even worn.'

She dragged me down the street and into the shop where the girls got busy searching the rails. Old jumpers, shirts, trousers, nothing that looked vaguely wearable for a catwalk.

'Are you looking for anything in particular?' asked the white-haired lady behind the counter.

'A size ten couture dress,' I said.

The lady smiled and didn't look as if I'd asked for anything out of the ordinary at all. 'You may be in luck, dear. My niece runs a vintage shop a few doors down. It's closed for refurbishment but she dropped a few things off here as I have plenty of storage. Hold on, I've got them round the back.'

Moments later, she returned with an armful of old dresses. Brightly coloured fifties style that would look totally out of place on the catwalk. We sifted through and sighed. None of them were anywhere near right.

'I have to go, Pia,' I said. 'If I'm not back, I'll be out.'

'Hold on a second,' said the shop lady. 'There's one more.'

She disappeared again and came back with a dress that was covered in plastic. She pulled it out.

'Oh my God,' said Pia. 'It's perfect!'

It was the most beautiful long bronze silk dress with criss-cross panels over the torso and it flared out at the bottom. 'It's vintage Dior,' said the lady. 'It would look lovely with your chestnut hair.'

'Quick, try it on,' said Meg.

'And I'll go and catch your gran. I can see her outside the other shop. I'll get her to go and bring the car,' said Pia.

I raced to the changing room, tore off my jeans and jumper and put the dress on. It fitted like a dream. I pulled the curtain back so that Meg and Flo could see.

'Wow!' said Meg.

'Totally,' said Flo. 'It makes your figure look fantastic, like it was made for you.'

I glanced at my watch. Twenty-five minutes left. 'OK. Got to go.' I quickly changed back and went over to the counter. How much is it?'

'Eight hundred pounds,' said the lady.

'*What!* Oh no!'

'How much do you have?'

'Fifteen pounds.'

'And I could put in four,' Flo offered.

'And me five,' said Meg.

'So that means we're . . . seven hundred and seventy-six pounds short,' I said.

The lady laughed. 'Oh dear. Is it for a special occasion?'

I nodded. 'A teen model competition. All the dresses for the show this evening have been supplied by up-and-coming designers. My dress went missing.'

'Is this the show with Tanisha?' asked the old lady.

'That's the one.'

'I saw an article about it in the paper. Hold on a moment,' said the lady. 'I've got to make a call.'

'OK but we have to go. Thanks anyway for showing us,' I said. I knew I was running out of time.

'No. I mean *hold* on. I may be able to help,' said the lady. She went to the back of the shop and made a call. I heard her talking animatedly into the phone. Moments later, she was back with a big grin on her face. 'The dress is yours for the evening. Cinderella, you shall go to the ball. My niece has just asked that you return the dress, you look after it and that her shop gets a mention in the show's PR.'

'That won't be a problem,' said Flo. 'All the other suppliers have their names credited.'

A flash of concern crossed the lady's face. 'I . . . it's an expensive dress and I've only just met you. How do I know that I can trust you?'

Flo noticed that Gran had just drawn up outside. She ran out to talk to her. Moments later, Gran came into the shop.

'I'll leave my credit card,' she said. 'Will that do?'

The lady regarded Gran then nodded and turned to me. 'And give me your name and address.'

I quickly gave her my contact details. 'Oh God,

thank you, thank you. You're my fairy godmother,'
I said.

The lady glanced down at the paper I'd written on.
'Porchester Park?'

'Yes, my dad's the general manager there.'

The lady smiled then thrust the dress into my
hands. 'Good luck tonight. Is it open to the public?'

I nodded. 'Seven thirty.'

'I might just come along,' she said.

'Even better,' I said. 'Then I can give the dress
straight back to you.'

Pia nudged me. 'We have to go, Jess.'

I thanked the lady again then we raced to the car
and Gran drove like a maniac back to Atlas Buildings.
We made it with three minutes to spare.

18

The Finale

'Number six, *go*,' said Suzie.

We were halfway into the evening dress section of the catwalk show. We'd done the casual wear and, so far, the event was going brilliantly. Suzie had been delighted with the dress and given me permission to wear it. Even some of the contestants had come forward to say how perfect they thought it was. It had been a blur of activity since I arrived back at Atlas Buildings: make-up, hair, pep talk from Suzie, into our dresses as the audience were arriving in the main hall and then Tanisha had introduced the show wearing a stunning skintight gold evening dress. As always, she looked every inch the pop diva. The atmosphere was electric from the moment the doors had opened to the public and I was buzzing with excitement to be part of it.

As girl number six sashayed back up the catwalk, I peeked through the curtains. My lot were on row seven: Dad, Gran, Aunt Maddie, Pia, Flo, Meg Charlie, Henry and Alexei. I spotted Tom and a few boys from school a few rows behind them.

'Seven, go,' Suzie instructed and the athletic-looking black girl glided off. She looked lovely in a scarlet silk dress.

'Eight, get ready,' said Suzie.

Eight was me. I took a deep breath and took my place.

'Go,' said Suzie a few moments later. I took another deep breath and stepped out. Bright lights dazzled me as I walked along the walkway. *Steady*, I thought. *Remember everything you've been taught. Not too fast. Look ahead. Long steps. Stomp, end, pow.* When I reached the end of the catwalk, I did a quick pose with lots of attitude then glanced down at my row of supporters. Nine smiling faces beamed back at me. Dad gave me the thumbs up. *Brilliant*, I thought. I did a perfect spin and before I knew it, I was backstage with Suzie. It felt absolutely fanbloomintastic.

'Wow, that was amazing,' I said to the blonde girl who had been number six. She agreed and we stood to the side and watched the last few girls hit the runway. Everyone looked stunning. It would be hard to pick a winner.

In a short interval, while the judges counted votes, the audience got up to enjoy drinks and elegant snacks that were laid out at the back of the room. Pia appeared in the dressing room. She handed me a sandwich. 'Bet you're starving,' she said. 'Your gran sent this with strict instructions for you to eat every bite!'

Eating was the last thing I felt like doing but as I bit into the soft brown bread, tomatoes and cheese, I real-ised that Pia was right. I was starving. As I chewed, I noticed the security man who usually was at the front desk of the building had come in and was talking to Suzie. He handed her a small package. Suzie frowned as she listened to him then she looked over at me and then Keira.

Oh God, what now? I wondered as Suzie left with the security man. *Has Keira been brewing more trouble?*

Five minutes later, Suzie returned with Tanisha. They both looked very serious.

Tanisha clapped her hands. 'Girls, *girls*. I need you to pay attention,' she called. The room hushed and everyone turned to look at her.

'It's with great sadness that I have to say that one of you has been caught cheating.' A gasp of surprise filled the room. 'This person will be leaving the competition immediately.'

Everyone turned to look at each other. I felt a pain in the pit of my stomach and glanced over at Keira. Had she set me up? She looked deathly pale.

'I won't tolerate this kind of behaviour,' Tanisha continued. 'Modelling is hard enough and competitive enough without girls deliberately attempting to sabotage each other's chances.' She looked directly at Keira who wouldn't meet her eyes. 'One of the dresses was taken this morning before the final rehearsals. What the person who did this didn't realise is that the whole building is covered by discreet CCTV. She was clearly seen—'

Keira didn't wait to hear any more. She bolted for the door but three girls blocked her way. She resisted briefly and try to get past them then collapsed in a heap on the floor.

'Get out of your dress, collect your things and go NOW,' Tanisha ordered.

Keira got to her feet and shot me a look of pure hate as she crossed the silent room. She grabbed her bag then headed for the cloakroom. No-one said anything as she skulked away.

When she'd gone, Tanisha smiled. 'Now, girls,' she said. 'I don't want this incident to spoil what has been a great night so, touch up your make-up and get ready to go back out to face the judges as soon as the band have finished. Good luck and remember, you're all winners. To have come so far out of so many girls and to have stayed the course, takes a brave heart as well as a beautiful face.'

'See you out front,' Pia whispered. 'Good luck.'

I did as Tanisha had instructed and retouched my make-up. As joined the line of girls getting ready to go back out for the final parade, I didn't know what to think or feel. Keira had been rotten to me, no doubt about that, but she'd been caught and humiliated in front of everyone and I couldn't help but feel sorry for her.

Out front, the audience were seated once again and there was applause as spotlights flashed onto the judges and Tanisha as they took their places behind a table to the right of the stage. The lights dimmed then came up again as the girl band, the Righteous Angels, blasted into a number.

'God, the suspense is killing me,' whispered the blonde girl with the heart-shaped face.

'I know,' I said. I loved the Righteous Angels but I just wished they would finish and we could get on.

After what seemed like an eternity, but was in fact only two songs later, the band took a bow and left the stage. *Show-time*, I thought and I tensed myself for the countdown.

An upbeat soundtrack began to play and the nine remaining contestants sashayed out. I couldn't resist and did a little jig step in time to the music and the audience laughed.

The music stopped and we all lined up to face the audience. Tanisha stood up and thanked everyone for coming. 'And so at last, we have our winner. As you can see, it's been a hard decision as each and every one of these girls in front of you is beautiful. But it's a contest and the public have made their votes. The winner will go on to do the summer cover of *Teen in the City* magazine and win the prize of five thousand pounds. And the winner is . . .'

I swear I could hear the pounding heart of every girl in the line-up as we waited to hear. After an agonising pause, Tanisha announced, 'Misaki Neiii.'

The entire two rows behind my friends and family burst into applause and stood up, followed by the rest of the audience. Tanisha beckoned her forward and Misaki went to claim her prize while all the contestants clapped and cheered. Some girls looked disappointed and couldn't hide it, most seemed genuinely glad. Misaki was a sweet girl and was a popular choice. I looked at my friends and family. Gran made a face as if to say, never mind. I didn't. The whole night had been a blast but I knew deep inside, that as far as modelling went, I wasn't in it for life like some of the others.

Music began to play again and all the girls began to bop along, as the audience below cheered and some people even got up and danced along with us.

Meg, Flo, Pia, Henry, Charlie and Gran were all up on their feet, but further back, I noticed that Tom looked puzzled. He must have been wondering where Keira was. Pia turned around and saw him. She got up and went back to him. I could see by the angry expression on his face that she'd told him what had happened.

As I left the building with my friends and family, Tom was standing at the bottom of the steps having a heated conversation with Keira. There was no other way out so we had no option but to walk past.

'Are you happy now you got me thrown out?' Keira snarled.

'I think you got yourself thrown out,' said Pia. 'You stole the dress, not Jess.'

Keira's face filled with rage. 'God. You are all so not worth me wasting any more time on.' She went to link arms with Tom. 'Come on, we're leaving.'

Tom shook her off. 'I don't think so,' he said and joined our group.

Keira was lost for words and I could almost see steam coming out of her ears. She pulled the collar on her jacket up and stomped off down the road in the opposite direction.

Tom looked embarrassed. 'You looked really good up there tonight, Jess,' he said and gestured in the direction Keria had gone. 'And . . . and I'm sorry about her.'

I shrugged. 'Actually, I feel a bit sorry for her.'

'Are you disappointed you didn't win?' he asked.

'No, honestly,' I said. 'Though I suppose the prize money would have been nice. In fact, I'm looking forward to putting catwalks and everything to do with them firmly behind me.'

Pia laughed. 'Fat chance. Don't forget we have the show to do for school in a month!'

19

Catwalk Show Mark Two!

It was a week before the catwalk show at school and I'd had an idea. I'd talked it over with Pia and she suggested that I showed Tanisha and invited her.

'Let's really go for it,' said Pia.

'Do you think she'd come?' I asked. Our school wasn't exactly the kind of glamorous location Tanisha was used to. 'And Dad might object.'

Amazingly, Dad gave me permission to ask Tanisha and I went up there completely ready for her to show me the door.

She glanced through my proposal then let out a low whistle.

Oh dear, I thought, *she's not going to buy it.*

'OK. Different. So . . .' Tanisha started then gave me a big grin. 'I'm in.'

The scene was set. The lights were low in the school hall and the audience were filtering in to take their seats to the background sounds of a chill-out CD that Charlie had put on the sound system.

Backstage our fifteen models were getting ready.

'All set?' asked Tanisha.

I gave her the thumbs up. My team had been brilliant. Charlie on sound, Henry and JJ on lights, Meg, Pia and Alisha on costumes. Flo and I had worked with the models showing them everything we'd learnt from the contest about attitude, posture and walking.

When everyone was in the hall, the lights went out and a murmur ran through the audience. No doubt wondering why they were sitting in pitch-darkness.

Charlie replaced the music track with a CD that we'd made in the previous week of girls in our school answering a question that had been asked of them. Meg, Pia, Flo and I had collected all the answers over the last few weeks then edited them. Sound bite after sound bite. The question we'd asked them was how did they feel about their image and was there anything

216

they didn't like about the way they looked. The CD began to play.

'I hate my ears, I look like a monkey.'

'My bum is *gross*.'

'I hate my shape. I look like a boy.'

'I'm too top heavy.'

'I have no boobs. I'd have surgery if I could.'

'I hate my nose.'

'I loathe my thighs, they're way too big.'

'My hair is a nightmare. Frizz city.'

'My legs are too skinny.'

'I have enormous feet, out of proportion to the rest of me!'

We let it play for a few minutes. The lights turned up a little and I peeped out at the audience as the sound bites continued. The audience had tittered nervously at first then looked puzzled, still not sure what was going on.

'God I hope this works,' I said to Flo.

'It will. It will be fine,' she replied.

'What gave you this idea, Jess?' whispered Tanisha as the CD played on.

'It was weeks ago. I'd been talking with my mates and we all had something we hated about ourselves. Tummy, bum, hair, teeth – just like the girls talking on the CD. I was amazed. I thought I was the only one who was down about my looks. So we went around the whole school with a recorder and asked, what don't you like about the way you look? *No-one* hesitated in replying, even the most stunning girls.'

'Me too,' said Tanisha. 'I never liked my butt.'

Amazing, I thought, Tanisha looked perfect to me but like the rest of us, she had her hang-ups.

As the CD continued, I checked to see if our models were ready, lined up behind me. They were.

'Go,' I said into my phone to Henry then I turned to the girls and beckoned them forward. Spotlights hit the stage as our girls walked out. All fifteen were dressed top to toe in grey lycra, no make-up, hair either tied or gelled back, each one of them wearing an exaggerated body part. Phoebe Miller from Year Ten was wearing enormous ears; after her, Lucy Green, Year Nine, with a prosthetic huge bum; Sally Cassidy, from Year Eleven, followed with big false boobs strapped to her chest; following her – Jackie Heller, Year Eight, with enormous feet; after her, Kassandra Taylor, Year Ten, with big hands; Tasha Booth, Year Seven, with an enormous nose; Alice Denton, Year Ten, with a huge padded stomach, I quickly donned a wig that looked like a bird's nest. And so the soundtrack of answers continued:

'My hair's a frizzy mess.'

'My hair's too limp and I hate my teeth.'

'I do NOT like my calves.'

'I'm getting a bit of a belly because I haven't any time to get to the gym! I also don't like my belly button!'

'I don't like my double chin, it makes my face look fat.'

The audience burst into laughter as the models paraded around, some of them making sad faces to go with the sad comments.

'I dislike my stomach. Eugh. I hate how I get spots and am fat.'

'I'm too skinny and my legs are like sticks!'

'I dislike *everything* about myself.'

'I hate to look at myself because I think I'm not pretty as everyone else.'

'I hate how my skin is pale.'

'I HATE my skin and my stomach. It won't get flat no matter how healthy I eat or how much I work out.'

'I hate my big nose.'

'I feel I'm fat like a cow.'

'I hate my weight, my nose, my teeth, my acne, my ears, my hair. Lots more. How long have you got?'

'I don't like my pale complexion. People often stop me and ask me if I'm all right. People call me the ghost.'

'Give me that butt,' said Tanisha as Lucy came off with the big bum. Lucy whipped it off and gave it to Tanisha who strapped it to her behind. I put on a pair of huge breasts. 'Let's go, girl,' said Tanisha to me.

The audience gawped in surprise as Tanisha and I trooped on. We did our best miserable faces and the audience laughed again. As we left the stage, Tanisha took off the plastic bottom and went and took her place centre stage, and a spotlight hit her. Like all our models, she was in plain grey lycra with her hair pulled back, but somehow she still managed to exude glamour.

'Good evening and welcome,' she said. 'Tonight we're looking at the idea of beauty. The voices you've just been listening to were those of girls here at this school. Seems *no-one* is happy with their lot. Too fat, too thin, too short, too tall, too curvy, not enough curves, I hate my hair, I hate my nose, my butt, my tummy. *On* it goes. We do what we can, don't we, girls? We crash diet, we starve ourselves, have hair extensions, use straighteners, some even resort to plastic surgery and implants in a quest to find our perfect self but only too often, we feel we don't make the grade – that we aren't and never will be beautiful. And yet around the world, the idea of beauty changes from culture to culture, did you know that?' She indicated a screen at the back of the stage and nodded at Henry and JJ who were positioned at the back of the hall behind the projector. The lights dimmed again and images began to appear on the screen from countries around the world.

'In some cultures, to be big is a sign of wealth and health. The bigger, the better, the more beautiful,' Tanisha read from my script as images of women in Mauritania appeared. 'In Africa, the Kayan tribe women wear brass rings from the age of five – the longer the neck, the more attractive they're considered to be.' Images of women with elongated necks wearing numerous brass necklaces appeared. 'This is also a tradition of the Pa Dong tribe on the Thai/Burmese borders. To the Maori tribe in New Zealand, to have full blue lips is a sign of beauty and they tattoo their lips and chins. Odd you think? They may think the same about how we choose to paint our lips red or pink here in the West.' Images of women from Maori with blue lips appeared followed by images of Western women with bright red lips. 'In Ethiopia, women of the Karo tribe wear scars on their stomachs to attract husbands. These are just a few examples but enough to see that external beauty is an individual, subjective concept,' Tanisha continued, 'what one culture finds beautiful, another might find outrageous, weird, even ugly.' Images continued on the back screen. Different countries, different styles. 'And not even from country to country. Just look back at history in the West and we laugh at the fashions and what was considered to look good.' Images from the past appeared, medieval times, Georgian times, pale ladies with wigs piled high on top. Image after image, showing changing fashions through time. Afro perms from the nineteen sixties, then hair that was short then long then short again.

'The boys did a great job,' Pia whispered as we watched. I nodded but we'd all contributed, sending Henry, JJ and Charlie images that we'd found and wanted included. JJ had been a star and been down in the VIP shed with us most nights selecting shots. He had a good eye and clearly enjoyed getting the show ready as much as the rest of us. We'd had three dates since he'd been back from LA. One to the movies, along with Vanya, his minder. One to a lovely restaurant in Holland Park, also with the minder. We'd tried to dodge him so that we could continue our first kiss but he kept appearing. It was more than his job's worth to lose sight of JJ. For the third date, we got a takeaway and ate it in the VIP shed where we were finally allowed to be on our own. That was the best date and we talked until so late that Dad had to come and tell him to go home. We found we had so much in common although he had done so much more than me. I liked that. I felt I could learn from him as well as enjoy hanging out. We also talked about how we were going to be straight with each other about how we felt, no games, no pretending to be cool or indifferent. Best of all, we'd managed to kiss without anyone watching and whenever I thought about those times, it made my toes curl up.

Out front of stage, Tanisha laughed as images of mad fashions from the seventies showed on the screen. 'And how many times have we looked back at an old photo of ourselves and said, *Oh my God. How could I have worn that! Look at my hair!* I know I have. Fashion changes across the world as well as over time. But what is beauty? Is there a beauty that transcends both time and culture? Is there any hope for us girls who don't fit the latest look put out by the media? And yes, I mean me too. I was the ugly duckling at school. Too tall. Frizzy hair. Knock-kneed. My big ole butt. I've been there, believe me. We asked the girls here at school what *they* thought beauty was and this is what they said.'

The lights dimmed again. Charlie changed the CD to a gentle unobtrusive classical track and the voices of girls from the school corridors played across the PA again.

'Beauty comes from within.'

'Confidence in who you are is beauty.'

'Whenever I think of beauty I think about inner beauty – because that's the beauty that really matters, not how you look on the outside, all that's pointless if there is no beauty on the inside.'

As the girls' voices played, Henry switched on the next slide show. We'd been up all night looking for the rights shots for this section of the show. The first image was of a group of Indian women laughing, then image after image followed of faces showing joy. All ages, all cultures. There was no denying the light in the women's and girls' eyes and faces and the beauty that shone from within. After that were images of faces looking tender, looking at a child with love, or a lover with care. I wanted to put these shots in because I didn't want anyone to think that to be beautiful, you had to go around laughing like an idiot all the time. When my mum was dying, I met some truly beautiful people at the hospital. People who looked after her. And the look of care on their faces sometimes blew me away. It was truly beautiful.

The girls' voices continued. 'True beauty is finding strength in difficult situations.'

My favourite image flashed up. It was of Aunt Maddie sitting at my mum's bedside though you can't see Mum in the picture. I knew that when the photo was taken, Aunt Maddie'd just heard that there was nothing more that could be done for Mum, her sister. All Aunt Maddie felt is there in her face in the photo, an expression of such love and sadness as she looks down at my sleeping mother. Her spirit shining through.

The slide show moved on to more images of women around the world.

'Beauty is the way you think and how you express yourself. Your feelings!'

'If you think of yourself as beautiful, other people will also notice it – because beauty comes from the inside.' An image of a bunch of little girls all dressed for a party and looking proud as punch flashed up and the audience went, 'Ah.'

'I think beauty is being able to look at yourself and be perfectly happy with who you are. Being true to yourself.'

A great image of a Japanese girl dressed eccentrically showed up.

'For me, beauty is originality, eccentricity.'

'A beautiful girl is someone who accepts her own body, her face, her nationality. Someone who can walk on the street with her chin up.'

'Well, sadly, nowadays beauty is about a good haircut, a nice body, beautiful nails, cool clothing and make-up . . . but for me, a beautiful person is the one who's a wonderful friend who's always there for you.'

'Beauty isn't all about looks and how you put on your make-up on, it's about personality and being comfortable with who you are as a person.'

'When you see someone completely at ease with themselves and loving life that is truly beautiful.'

'Trying to be someone you're not, whether through clothes, make-up or personality, just doesn't work. It just makes you look and feel superficial. But being happy in your own skin, in your own life, lets the real beauty shine through!'

'Inner beauty is the most important! It doesn't have to do with your physical appearance. Unfortunately, thousands of people don't know that yet.'

'Happiness is the most important beauty product in the world.'

'Real beauty for me is love, whether it's friendship or love between two lovers, it doesn't matter.'

'It runs much deeper than just physical attraction and a pretty face.'

Quote after quote was played. I checked the audience. Many were nodding with agreement and approval.

'I think you get the picture,' said Tanisha with a smile. 'And remember, you heard it here, folks. Girls, don't waste your life wanting to be something you're not. Taller, shorter, thinner, blonde, paler, whatever. There's only one of you and you are just darn perfect. Unique. Don't miss your life putting yourself down because you think you need to lose, or put on, half a stone. I say strut what you got. There's *only* one of you. Celebrate that. Some of you may know that I've just mentored a modelling competition for the catwalk and we had many beautiful girls enter, but I'm so glad to be here too to see even more beautiful girls, girls who maybe don't fit the catwalk mould but are lovely just the same in their own way. I want to celebrate them too. See, we all know what's the truth deep down and the voice-over from the girls at the school here is testament to that despite the early answers about what they didn't like. OK, you can wear a bit of gloss, you can wear a pretty outfit, enjoy the fashion shown to us in magazines, but we all know what makes someone truly beautiful. Deep, deep down you know it's who you are inside. We know it so let's live it!'

Charlie flicked a switch and a funky upbeat track began to play. I checked to see if the models were ready again. They were. All lined up behind me. Chloe, the make-up artist from the previous show, had been a star and, as promised, had turned up earlier with a team. We'd discussed the look we wanted and the fifteen girls had been transformed from pale schoolgirls to bold, colourful warrior queens with dark eyes and gashes of colour on their faces.

'What is beauty?' Tanisha continued. 'I know the world of fashion and beauty and it's a wonderful world to work in. It is. It's creative, it's innovative and glamorous with some bright and fantastic people in it, but there are two sides, the good and bad. I also see girls starve themselves. I see girls have surgery. I see beautiful girls put themselves down if they gain a pound, they agonise about ageing. Believe me, what some of them put themselves through ain't pretty and in real life, most of them don't look the way they do in magazines. They get airbrushed to have flaw-less skin, cellulite is painted out, limbs lengthened to give this image of a perfect look we all aspire to and despise ourselves if we can't make it but it's *not* real.'

The upbeat soundtrack began to play as Tanisha and the models began to strut the catwalk. We'd had two rehearsals how to walk, stomp, pow and they'd caught on brilliantly. Each was wearing her favourite party outfit. First was Lucy Green. Size sixteen, she was sassy and gorgeous. After her was Phoebe, a tiny girl but she owned that runway. She was followed by Jackie who was tall and skinny – she danced down the catwalk. A cheer rang out from the audience as they got what we were trying to say. Girl after girl walked out, all shapes, all the different nationalities we had at the school, all hair colours.

'Are you going to go out again?' I asked Tanisha.

She shook her head. 'This part is your show.'

'There's a great atmosphere out there,' said Charlie as the girls came off to get changed into their casual outfits. 'At first, I thought everyone was going to laugh but I think they really get it.'

When the final outfits had been shown, everyone went out on the catwalk together. I beckoned the team down from the back so Flo, Meg, Pia, Charlie and Henry went out as well to rapturous applause. Alisha and JJ stayed backstage. They had come to the show incognito because they didn't want anyone getting wind of the fact that they were related to Jefferson Lewis and so steal the limelight. However, I noticed Alisha put on the orange wig, and JJ cracked up and put on another wig and some of the body parts. I got it. No-one would know it was them except the two minders who were also backstage. I beckoned JJ and Alisha to come out and even Tanisha couldn't resist and came to join us. The girls began to dance and very soon the audience were on their feet too, even Mrs Callaghan, our headmistress.

Result! I thought as I looked at the models. *No-one excluded, everyone included and that's exactly how it should be.*

The next morning, JJ was down having coffee with Charlie, Henry, Alexei, Pia, Flo and me and we'd been sitting around the breakfast bar munching muffins and posting photos from the school show on my laptop on Facebook. Flo and Charlie had got together at last. One night while working on the school show, Charlie had finally summoned the courage to tell her that he liked her. They'd had their first date last week and had a second one planned this evening. They both seemed so happy and right together at last. Flo had told Alexei she only wanted to be friends and he'd admitted that although he liked her, he hadn't felt ready for a committed relationship, so they were totally cool with each other, especially when he heard that we'd all promised to invite him around when we were hanging out. He'd told Flo that it meant a lot to him to be part of a group of mates.

The doorbell rang and Charlie went to answer. He came back moments later with a large bunch of white roses.

I glanced over at JJ. 'Thank you,' I said.

He looked puzzled. 'They're not from me, but hey, look, there's a note.'

'I bet they're from Tanisha,' said Pia as she picked out the card. 'She really enjoyed last night.' She read the card. 'Oh my God!'

What?' asked JJ.

He took the card before Pia could stop him then passed it to me.

Dear Jess, you're right. I AM a player. Have been a player. Was a player. It's in the past. No more games. We

231

do have something special and I don't want to blow it. You're the One. And I'm yours if you still want me. Tom

JJ looked down at my laptop. 'Got his email address on there?'

I nodded.

He went to my mail and found Tom's email address.

He quickly typed in a message that I just had time to read before he pressed send. It said: **As you Brits say, too late, mate. She's taken. JJ Lewis.**

He raised an eyebrow at me, smiled and put his hand over mine. I had a proper boyfriend at last.

If you love

Million Dollar Mates

and can't wait to see what Jess does next . . . Look out for the next book in the series, *Golden Girl,* coming soon!

About the Author

Cathy Hopkins lives in Bath, England with her husband and three cats, Dixie, Georgia and Otis. Cathy has been writing since 1986 and started writing teenage fiction in 2000. She spends most of her time in her writing turret pretending to write books but is actually in there listening to music, hippie dancing and checking her facebook page. So far Cathy has had fifty three books published, some of which are available in thirty three languages.

She is looking for the answers to why we're here, where we've come from and what it's all about. She is also looking for the perfect hairdresser. Apart from that, Cathy has joined the gym and spends more time than is good for her making up excuses as to why she hasn't got time to go. You can visit her on Facebook, or at www.cathyhopkins.com